EXES

MAX WINTER
EXES

CATAPULT
NEW YORK

The characters in this book are fictitious. Any similarity to real persons, living or dead, is coincidental and not intended by the author.

Published by Catapult
catapult.co

ISBN: 978-1-936787-40-1

Catapult titles are distributed to the trade by
Publishers Group West
Phone: 800-788-3123

Library of Congress Control Number: 2016940589

Printed in the United States of America

9 8 7 6 5 4 3 2 1

For Olivia

Only the notebooks of my antiquarian uncle . . . revealed to me at length the darker, vaguer surmises which formed an undercurrent of folklore among old-time servants and humble folk; surmises which never traveled far, and which were largely forgotten when Providence grew to be a metropolis with a shifting modern population.

—H. P. Lovecraft

Everything should be kept. I regret everything I've ever thrown away.

—Richard Hell

Contents

EXES

Side by Each

Clay Blackall III

My landlord didn't want to call the cops. For five years he'd been shuffling me from empty place to empty place while he fixed up the thirty or so eyesores my grandfather sold him. He felt bad about my brother, but bad only gets you so far. Smith Hill was the end of the line. Two babies had fallen out of windows that year alone, and now a guy was walking around with a sword. If you touched the stove and the refrigerator at the same time, you got a shock that felt like a punch in the heart. I'd wet my hands and grab hold and come to in another room.

I told him I needed one more month—for Eli—and he just shook his head.

"I could get six bills for this place, easy," he said. "Seven even." He cracked a window, zipped his jacket. He went to open the kitchen cabinets, which held what one expects to find in kitchen cabinets, but also other things.

"Five years is a long time," one of us added.

"Ah, hell," my landlord said—in a different voice. He was breathing through his nose, for one thing. "Your grandpa used to tell me I was like a Jew. 'Luongo,' he would say, 'in my eyes, you're a

Jew.' And from him, I took it. 'I'll take it,' I'd say, like it was the first time he told me." His eyes were wet, like men's sometimes get near the end. He toed an unplugged cord to see where it led and shook his head when he did. "Jesus, Clay, this is your icebox. You were supposed to take care of things, keep an eye out."

"That's two different jobs," I said.

A couple minutes later, and he was still shaking his head. I watched him through the bedroom window. For two blocks I could hear his truck rattle. No wonder Grandpa Ike liked him. He'd always known his grandkids weren't cut out for the family business, but still.

My kid brother Eli's first car crash into that house at the foot of Jenckes had wiped out his inheritance. His second crash wiped out mine. Now I only had a month or so left of walking-around money, and another year of eating money, maybe. But if I also had to make rent, forget it. Our sister, Libby, was doing okay, I guess, but I hadn't seen her since Eli's shivah. "This is my fault?" I asked when she made it clear she didn't want to hug me.

"I was here for him," she said. "Where were you?"

"He didn't want to see me," I said. I thought about it. "I reminded him of him?"

"Eli looked up to you."

"He hated mirrors," I said, touching the sheet on the one in the hall.

"Why can't you see things for what they are?" she said, making a face that even I could get.

And now it had been five years. How many Mays are there in five years? May is always hard, but this one was cold and wet, like March. Maybe this was just what spring is for us now.

Luongo said I had a week to clear out and I could use the dumpster. So even though I didn't know where I was going, I got going. It took two days. First I gathered what I needed—meaning everything I had about Eli, which wasn't nearly enough, but also underwear and my dead father's metal detector, the only *thing* he left me. Then I burned any documents I didn't need but also didn't want anyone to find in an old oil drum out back. I fed the fire with exed-out calendars and gas station porn that had long since ceased to do the trick. It burned green. I poked at it with a stick and took pulls off an ass pocket of red-hot schnapps I found under the sink—ginger, maybe, or cinnamon? In the dumpster, I threw things no one would want, no matter what mind they were in. The rest I left where it was or else put curbside. I swept the apartment. I swept and I swept and I swept, stopping now and then to clean the bristles. Dust is intimate. From under the couch I swept genetic information. From under the bed I swept Kleenex and the bits of glass that hadn't wound up in my heel. From under the icebox I swept magnets, third and final notices, cards for unkept appointments with people who knew they couldn't help me, and a yellowed *Yankee Swapper* clipping:

> CARETAKER WANTED: Twinrock is a century-old summer cottage atop rock in Narragansett Bay. From Fall to Spring. No charges. 17 rooms. Fully stocked larder. No heat. No potable water. Some upkeep. Working knowledge of plumbing, carpentry, wiring, and masonry preferred. Must be able to swim and understand tides, storms and surges. Should cope well with solitude. No guests/pets. Contact Fud Mays at ███-████.

Fud Mays's niece was Eli's ex, Alix. As far as I know, Eli spent only one awful night at Twinrock, but still. I affixed the ad to the fridge with the least greasy magnet and got started on the bathroom. I took off the shower curtain. I poured bleach and shuffled a towel around. I blinked at the clock. It was almost light out. I put on a sweater and smashed the clock with a hammer. I swept it up and shut the windows.

The metal detector just fit in the trunk of my grandfather's last Skylark. I liked to leave the passenger seat empty, because you never know. The backseat had been full for some time. Twice a year, at least, our late mother would hand us two Almacs bags apiece and lock us into our rooms until we filled them. Eli, I would later learn, buried what he couldn't part with in a secret spot beneath a terminal tower in nearby India Point Park—the nose glasses Mother hated, and the matchbooks and swizzle sticks our great-uncle Charles would mail us on holidays, but also his invisible friends: a pair of twins named Furry and Furry.

It was a Thursday; Friday was trash day. But it was early enough that folks would still get a crack at things they might want. "Hey neighbors," I yelled. "Help yourself!"

A drunk on a bike coasted past. *"Arrivederci,"* he yelled back. His white T-shirt was gray and his white skin was red. His red hair, meanwhile, was white and mostly gone. "You white asshole," he added, turning the corner.

Determining which skiff belonged to Twinrock wasn't hard, because there was one with a flowerpot and a broken snare drum and a jar of pennies in it. A handpainted sign nailed to the skiff's bench read CAN YOU SWIM TO THE ROCK? IF NOT, WEAR A VEST, with an arrow pointing to where there were no vests. I lowered in my things, the water jugs, myself. I looked at the motor.

At camp, I had to start a boat once. I was seventeen, and covering waterfront rec for the normal counselor. The only kid who wanted to fish was a boy of nine or ten who had played a hot girl in the play the week before. After the show I'd overheard that normal counselor—who liked to pick fights with the Brits till they put sugar in his gas tank—say, "Fuck, man. I want to fuck Ethan Flashman," then take a two-minute piss off the deck while humming an already-old "Wish You Were Here." Back then, five years was a lifetime. As Ethan and I motored across the lake, I focused on the rudder and the throttle rather than on his knees, which were delicate but ashy. He caught a sunfish, and eventually I got a feel for the engine, but I wouldn't cast a line, and we never talked. The whole time, "I want to fuck Ethan Flashman" kept looping in my head in a voice that wasn't mine. Then, "Damn, damn, damn," in a voice that might've been, if I could sing.

After a couple of priming pumps and three quick yanks, the Twinrock skiff came to life. Just like a lawn mower. Eli's last job was yard worker. One time I drove by a place where he was working. In my rearview mirror, Eli banged his weed whacker against the sidewalk five, six times, threw it into the street, and grimaced into his fist. I ran my errand. On my way back he was fixing the thing in the driveway, an unlit cigarette stuck to his lip. I should have said hi. Offered him a light? I could've pulled over.

For me the hardest part is forgetting things, but also not paying attention the first time around. My car was parked in the brambles at the edge of a nearby land trust, and no one would find it until late fall, if I wanted. I closed my eyes and listened to the outboard. I let out the choke. Then I undid the rope and motored out to the house on the rock, which sat a couple hundred yards from the shore of Bull Point.

The rock was twice as wide as the house and half as tall. The house was three gray stories of sea-beaten shingle, and looked like someone had lived in, built, and designed it, in that order. I lashed the boat to the dock with a made-up knot, doubled up and irreversibly tangled, and took the rear steps to the cellar. From the door hung a frowning woman's head in terra-cotta. She was an unsettling shade larger than life, and you could see the sculptor's fingertips, rough and quick and deep, in her clenched jaw. I tried the knob, but the door was locked, and now it was fully dark. I tasted my breath and looked for a likely looking rock, the kind people hide keys under.

There were little rocks everywhere, of course, but an especially heavy and flat-bottomed one that had once been painted white caught my eye. It had since been repainted to look like a rock again, complete with dirt and moss and trompe l'oeil bird shit. Under it I found a marine-proof sleeve that held the hoped-for key. I slipped it out and tried the lock; the key wiggled fruitlessly. I looked around for a smaller lock, but found none. The wind picked up. I leaned into the door, but it wouldn't budge.

The clouds had blown away, and the moon was so full and low it almost felt like day for night. The French call it *la nuit Americaine* because they love our old movies exactly as much as we think they hate our new ones. I looked for a door, a window, a box—anything. My vision doubled and I lost my footing, so I sat down and breathed into an imaginary bag till I realized that whatever I was sitting on was far too pointy to be a rock. I stood up and there it was: a model of the house itself, snow-globe scaled and cast in greening bronze. Because that's exactly how these jokes work—the sort greenhorns won't get. I turned it over and found a locked trapdoor. I steadied my hand until the first key fit perfectly. Inside was yet another plastic sleeve that held a larger, more suitable-looking key.

The door to the big house opened with a gritty little click. Inside, I fumbled for a light and held the wall while I climbed the basement stairs, which curved and had a net for a banister. The house's interior walls were also shingled, so it looked like outside inside. Rooms whorled around and opened up into one another like nautiloid chambers radiating off the parlor, which had a ping-pong table where you'd expect a couch. Framed and taped-up articles about the house itself covered the walls in the kitchen and the dining room. They were varying shades of yellow and degrees of brittle. All but one of the clippings mentioned that Fud had been married four times, and featured slight variations on his punch-line-less joke: "They knew it wouldn't work when they realized that I loved Twinrock more than them." In the sole two-pager, his sister, Kit—Alix's mother—added, "Twinrock eats women." Above the mantel hung an enormous photo of the house itself, beneath which someone had taped a cardboard arrow that read YOU ARE HERE.

I looked around. It was the kind of house that had a cardboard shadow theater instead of a TV and, in the kitchen, a drawer full of scrimshaw "he's-at-homes."

The bookshelves held the collected mid-twentieth-century American notions of what the world was and had been up to that point, mostly in the form of field guides, incomplete encyclopedia sets, dog-eared fact books, and long-forgotten bestsellers you could tell had been read in the tub. The books leaned this way and that, in no discernible order, their spines bleached by the sun. Mixed in with these were thirty years' worth of caretaker logs, a manila folder of well-thumbed grant proposals from 1998, a stack of dot-matrixed school papers, a couple of diaries, and bundled dime-store composition books belonging to the sort of writer who writes the same story over and over in longhand, changing only unimportant details from draft to draft. There were also at least two boxes' worth of the self-published paperback *The House on the Rock*, an "intimate" history of Twinrock, by N. Hazard Aldrich, its cover a pen-and-ink illustration of the book's subject. TAKE ONE HOME! exhorted the shelf tag taped beneath a particularly long stretch of them. I selected one with a bookmark. In the blurry black-and-white photo that was the book's back cover, the author wore elbow and eye patches and smoked a pipe. As a boy, I had always thought it merely a matter of finding an area of expertise. My Twinrock. I read standing up:

> FROM ROUGHLY the Middle Pennsylvanian to the late nineteenth century of our current epoch, the now ironical Twinrock appeared as the slightly squatter of a more or less matching pair of granite outcroppings sitting side by side* just off the coast of Jamestown, Rhode Island, near the mouth of Narragansett Bay. (The original Conaticut Indian name for the chain of rocks is lost to history.) Regrettably, the rock's erstwhile twin was cannonballed into submarine rubble by army gunners stationed across the water.

The rambling, slate-roofed, and eponymously named house on the rock was built atop Twinrock in 1903 by family scion Rear Admiral J. Ambrose Mays, a former Know-Nothing gubernatorial candidate whose prior Jamestown retreat, Ewelysses, had been seized by the federal government in the expansion of nearby Fort Wetherill. Twinrock was the crusty sea captain's rebuke. "I will build it where no man can bother me," he said. "But where I can still keep an eye out if I want."

*Or *side by each*, as publicly or parochially schooled locals like to say.

I was about to settle into the parlor's least fragile chair with *The House on the Rock* when I realized its bookmark was an envelope addressed—incompletely and optimistically—to Twinrock, care of Eli's ex, Alix.

I held the letter up to the light. Someone had steamed it open and resealed it. Fud? Surely not Kit. Eli? I checked the date on the California postmark. Not Eli. It hurt to swallow. I tested a corner with my thumbnail, but my hand was so shaky that I risked tearing the flap.

I tucked the still-sealed letter back into the book and wiped my face with an antimacassar that stunk of mold and, oddly, gribenes. My left ear began to ring. Silvery little exes glimmered at my vision's periphery. I gripped the mantel and caught both my breath and my haggard reflection in the house's many windows. I remembered all those homes on the shore, sitting in plain view of lit-up Twinrock. I retrieved my flashlight and ran about the house flipping off switches and yanking cords.

The house was dark, and quiet. In my current state, I didn't trust myself with either the envelope or its contents. Who knows what I'd find. When had I last slept?

Twinrock's sole windowless room was a linen closet. I removed half the shelves and bedclothes in order to accommodate a lamp and a milking stool. To wind down before bed, I played Clue against myself. The set was cobbled together from multiple editions from different eras. It was short the rope, the knife, and the revolver; and Mr. Green had been replaced with a lucky Jew figurine. I made up the statistical loss of murder weapons by adding an equivalent number of rooms within the preexisting rooms with a chisel-tipped marker. Nevertheless, I quickly lost to myself by jumping to Colonel Mustard—whom I always blame—with the candlestick in the kitchen shitter. It was Green all along, with the same item in the hall closet.

I tried to sleep beneath a coonskin coat that smelled like a failed expedition, but every time I almost went under, I would see Eli and my old man, feel like I was falling, and jerk awake. My heart pounded and so did my head, which now also had N. Hazard Aldrich's voice in it, narrating through his pipe. I got up and worried at the envelope, turning it over and over in the lamplight. It could wait till daybreak. Until then, I settled into a wicker club chair with a view of the increasingly blue edge of the sky's predawn black. If I had a pipe, I'd've smoked it, offshore glow be damned. But I knew elbow patches were meant to cover holes. My old man had taught me that. I felt like his human time capsule. I let him fill me up.

Eli and I were both born at Lying-In Hospital and brought up in a crumbling Angell Street Victorian at the foot of College Hill, along with that leggy elder sister I'll go some lengths not to discuss. But in the spring of 1974, when I was eleven and Eli seven, our father crashed his plane—a fork-tailed doctor killer that also held his wife, our mother—into the choppy waters off Block Island's southeast shore. The official story was a freak storm, but I later learned, thanks to my parents' lawyer, that in the air Father liked to pass around a bottle of Calvados. I wasn't surprised. Pa always did dig *le trou normand* and, from lunch on, favored pullovers, slip-on loafers, and pants with hidden elastic. Mother, meanwhile, locked up the lawn darts and, over her husband's slurred cheers of encouragement, scolded us down from steep, slippery things. By bathtime matters only worsened: "Look, boy," Pa would say, teetering on the tub's edge and pointing toward the vanity, where his open-gowned wife readied herself for bed and five-six minutes of coitus. "Your mother's beaver."

On his mother's side, Father was a direct descendant of Rhode Island's founder, Roger Williams. Our mother, meanwhile, was a second-generation Russian Jew, daughter of a local slumlord, Ike Hafkin, who made his nest egg renting triple-decker tenements the color of restaurant mints and worn-out dog noses.

Father's decision to wed a Jewess vexed the Blackalls and Hafkins alike, though for opposite reasons. So much so, that my parents quickly—and, in my mother's case, temporarily—found themselves cut out of their respective inheritances. Father increased his drinking and his tinkering commensurately. Few know that the basement-workshop-perfected formula for the popular sports drink/pediatric hydration therapy that would eventually earn my father his personal fortune had in fact been conceived of as a hangover cure for unathletic adults like himself. (Apple brandy is a son of a mothereffer the morning after, and, drunk or not, backyard catch with Pa was a farce.) But Eli and I both like to call in sick and sweat it out with a cup or two of hot black coffee, seeing hangovers as both inevitable and edifying.

Liked. I mean, *he* liked to.

I looked out the window. The sky was nearly blue. My quiet little sighs come from the Hafkin side of me; a Blackall sigh is strictly rhetorical.

Speaking of genes, young Eli, who from Father inherited far more than senatorial good looks, spent the entire weekend of our parents' funeral tucked into the uppermost crotch of a crabapple, where, clad in his favorite yellow swim trunks, he took quick, eye-crossing sips from a pilfered fifth of Pomerol. "But it makes me vanish," he told Libby when she had climbed up and said, "That's enough now" and "Come on—give it." Then she sat beside him while he combed her long blond hair with a pink pocket comb, now and then lifting loose golden strands from its wide plastic teeth and balling them into his pocket. Libby balls, Eli called them. He kept them under his pillow.

As soon as my parents were in the ground, Eli, Sis, and I went to live in Grandpa Ike and Grandma Tillie's colonial just off Hope on the East Side's easternmost side.

But Dad's folks could hold a grudge like you read about. After their only son's death, Bink and Meezy had little to do with any of us, least of all Coney Island–looking me. In fact, the only physical evidence—apart from a long-since-destroyed ER chart—that my father's parents were ever charged with our care is the framed snapshot that I brought with me. In it Eli (five?) and I (that makes me nine) sit astride a beloved roan mare, Abigail, precariously occupying the same pair of tooled leather chaps that, minutes prior to the camera's click, Pappy Bink had taken down from the wall of his den in a fit of gin-fueled hysterics. "Meezy! Look!" he'd cried. "They'll each get a leg!" We blink into the low Newport sun, hot, frowning, scared, and looking, despite our age gap, like the ethnically split halves of a single Judeo-Christian self: Eli, the fair-haired, long-limbed, sun-bronzed Viking; and me, a freckled little cartoon. To my knowledge, this is the only photograph of Eli and me that still exists. The nag threw us shortly thereafter, and I landed atop my little brother, breaking his arm. Pappy didn't take us to the naval hospital until the following morning, when, over flakes and juice, Eli continued to complain of the pain in his now strangely angled ulna. "Christ," Pappy muttered, loading us all into the Estate Wagon one last time.

• • •

The sun was nearly up when I remembered the boat. The neighbors and boatyard employees would almost certainly notice its absence from the dock and call Fud or send someone to check the house.

Flashlight in my mouth, I raided the armoire in the master bedroom for a suitable disguise should I be spotted at the skiff's helm, and found a dingy oxford, a pilled crewneck, a jacket lined with a tasteful pattern you couldn't see, pants made of an ugly one you could, and, finally, the obligatory ball cap faded the red of overcooked lobster shells. Shit, I thought. Shit. Shit. Shit. Shit.

In the near dark, I slid the jon boat from the basement and into the water, lashing it to the skiff with a heart-size knot. I motored back to Bull Point. At the shore, I undid the knot then retied the line to the dock, doubling and redoubling it till it was the size an owl, then a newborn child, and finally a Christmas ham. I rowed back to the rock, panting. The sky was bluer than seemed possible. Whatever shorebirds were the first ones up squawked at one another. The crewneck smelled like cheese and hormones. It smelled like me.

Before I knew it, I'd passed three full weeks alone in the house on the rock, but that didn't mean I couldn't find ways to get in my own way. A mere week in, I cut my foot on the sweat-honed toe crease of an unlost sock. (I only had two pair.) No aspirin. I sucked on spice drops pried from the roof of a hard-to-date gingerbread house. Mohels insist that sugar is an anesthetic, but they also think their mouths are antiseptic, so I chased the gumdrops with slugs of rum—Eli's drink of choice. Or was at one point, at least. We'd lost touch for a good ten years after he got fired for fucking his favorite high school student—but not because of that, as he and others thought. Quite the opposite, in fact. I wanted to hear all about it. About Alix. Even that bothered him.

But five Mays ago, Eli drove his car into that house at the foot of Providence's steepest street for the second and last time. He was thirty-three.

And although, that time, the house *did* belong to a former student's mother, it did not, as some still insist, belong to the mother of Eli's aforementioned favorite. The first time he had driven into the house, some nine years earlier, he had meant to hit the place right next door, which belonged to some rich lady who wouldn't let him use the can. (He had spent the entire workday in her yard, yanking weeds and planting standards.) But the two houses—Victorian twins sitting side by each, one putty, the other gray—are hard to tell apart at night. And the second time around, Eli had been mad only at himself and so hopeless that any old house at the foot of Jenckes would do. The car was an all-but-rusted-out Plymouth Volare he had bought minutes earlier from his upstairs neighbor for all the money he had, which wasn't much. The news split me in two. One of me stayed in bed, and the other one walked around, kept busy, got into trouble. We keep doubling back.

While my sister and I had attended the Amos Fox School, a local Quaker Friends prep of some renown, Eli had been homeschooled, against the wishes of the state and his grandparents—who, as soon as they had some say in the matter, enrolled him in a public elementary. "Maybe Clay Two, maybe he could make a go of it with this one, rest his soul, but me, what do I know from English?" Grandpa Ike said. And Eli did okay at MLK and elsewhere, but even so, upon graduating college, he took a job at Fox and began the impossible task of making up for lost time. He used to pore over Libby's and my yearbooks as if they were Christmas circulars.

Now, out on the rock, it was nearly June, and still, no visitors. But I couldn't get too comfortable. Athletic blondes, back home from college, spent whole afternoons dangling their legs from nearby diving docks and indulging in all manner of catalog-model horseplay. Back on land, scotch was being swapped out for gin. Sleeveless shifts and go-to-hell slacks were getting unmothballed. I had nowhere left to hide.

I tried my damnedest to graph Eli's last ten years, but couldn't. Truth was, I had no idea what *my* decade looked like, let alone his. I spread out. Back when I paid taxes, my tax man used the floor as his filing cabinet. Each client got a pile. "This poor lady," he'd say, pointing at a tilted stack of manila folders. "She's in real trouble." Now I made piles of my documents, too. Except each pile was a person Eli might've known, or known to say hi to. I spread them out, these exes, friends, and neighbors. These stand-ins and one-night stands, body doubles and doubles. I mixed them up. I filled in gaps with facts and news items. I used scissors. For glue, I used local honey. I stacked them back up. If I squinted, the piles looked like people.

Against my better judgment I started using one of the many taped-off toilets that flushed directly into the bay, rather than the composting model in the master bath. I was already off schedule, so generally it wasn't too hard to wait until after dark or just before sunup. But one morning, less than an hour after I pushed my luck on a can of expired hash, I heard knocking, and *hi there–ing* and *yoo-hooing* and *anybody-homing*. I stumbled, knocked things from shelves, fell down the stairs and up them. I hid in the cellar, then in the closet, then under the kitchen sink. There was even more knocking and anybody-homing, and then the door opening, and more and louder yoo-hooing and all manner of ayyy-upping and sports whistling. The intruder tramped around the house, picking up odds and ends, setting them down too hard. Opening cupboards. Rifling.

His weight strained the floorboards, and I all but smelled how he shaved. The door under the sink creaked open. Top-Siders with salt in their cracks, socks made of hairless skin.

"Hi there!" he yelled.

I reached into my pocket for the ball cap but found only snack wrappers. I rolled out from under the sink, spending more time than I'd've liked to on my back. He put out his hand, but I picked myself up. Now we were face-to-face. My back was against the sink, and he didn't step back. "Howdy," I managed.

"Frank," he said, extending once more his hand. It looked strong, and good at knots. "Frank Duffy."

I took it. "Eli," I said without thinking. "Hafkin." It felt good just to say it.

"I know you," he said, squeezing. "Fud around?"

"No." I took my hand back.

"A little early in the season for guests, isn't it?"

"Guest!" I said too loudly. "Ha! I'm the plumber. I've come to fix the sink." I pointed to my hiding spot, noticing—at the same time as he did, I'm guessing—the lack of tools.

"The plumber?"

"Yes, my toolbox is back on land. Left it behind like a regular idiot!"

"I'll take you ashore," he said, putting his hand on my shoulder and giving me a little push out of the kitchen.

I stumbled. "Oh, boy," I said, grabbing the metal detector case on the way through the living room. "It's my whattayoucallit . . . my snake."

"Sure thing, Clay."

I turned around and looked at him. He looked back like a print-ad cowboy looking at something far off.

"I knew your old man," he said. "Through the law office."

"Fishing?" I asked, smelling something on his boat.

"False albacore," he said, his eyes crinkling at the far dock now, like a cowboy sailor. "The gals in the office love it."

There was a cruiser waiting for me onshore. "You Claiborne Blackall?" the woman cop asked me.

"The Third?" added the man cop with a voice that smirked. His face did nothing.

I nodded.

"You're going to have to come with us," she said, taking the metal detector.

"Okay," I said.

"Is this a weapon, Clay?"

"No, ma'am," I said, looking at my store shoes, brown with worn-out soles, and at Fud's ill-fitting cords, mine now, that whisked when I walked. "Metal detector."

"You're a real creep, you know that?" the man cop said. My stomach was in my throat.

"Watch your head," the woman said. Then she eased me into the car and shut the door behind me. The backseat was hard, hollow plastic, like the seat of a Big Wheel or Green Machine, and I slid from one side to the other and slammed into the windows when we took corners. We took them hard. "It's slippery back there," she said. "You might want to hold on to something."

I was about to say *I am*, but caught myself. "I will," I said, and held on tighter.

Aloha

Vince Vincent

HI ALIX (IF THIS IS YOU),

YOU DON'T KNOW ME, BUT THAT'S NOT IMPORTANT. I FOUND THIS IN SOME PANTS VINCE LEFT AT MY PLACE AND THOUGHT WHAT THE HELL? HOPE THIS FINDS YOU.

NOBODY BELIEVED ME WHEN I TOLD THEM WHO I COULD'VE been, so I started pretending I was Judge Reinhold instead. This they believed. *Hey, I know that dude*, they'd think or say. It didn't even matter that we actually look alike, because they barely remembered how he looked then, let alone now. No, it worked mostly because when I watched that one scene I was thinking the same exact thing they were: that should be me.

In Hollywood we use hot actresses instead of seasons to measure time because every month is cruel, and hot, and dry. Except for when it's cold as hell. We're up by five and home by seven and drunk by eight. In bed by nine or ten. At dawn your next-door neighbor scoots to his car like he just committed a crime. Nothing is on the way to anything and everything is an hour away. It's neither here nor there, and there's no *here* here, either. We're all just brains for our cars. Or something our cars ate and can't digest. They call where I live now the desert. But isn't it *all* the desert? All I know is I'm finally far enough away from a 24 Hour Fitness to void my contract, and that I'd called L.A. home for as long as I could.

It's been more hot actresses than you can name since I could even read for a lead, let alone get called back. The last time was for the role of Brad Hamilton in *Fast Times at Ridgemont High*, which wasn't Judge Reinhold's yet. We were the same type, of course, but they went with him, because who knows? The whole thing took so long to not work out that the casting director felt bad, and gave me Brad's Bud #2. Then the DP pointed out that people might mistake us for brothers, and my scenes got cut.

It's okay, I thought. I'll get 'em next time, not knowing that next time meant the boyfriend part in a music video for a singer too old to play himself. Then came the cool dude from work in a sitcom that never got picked up. I got mugged in unconvincing lighting. I shouted funny drink orders in quiet clubs. Twice I played a corpse. But mostly I got by with embarrassing print ads. I gaped at home computers, threw footballs to pretend sons, and pointed at things you couldn't see in denim outfits.

People used to stop me on the street or in parking lots to ask if I was that guy, you know—what's his name? Oh, you know . . . I'd just smile and wave to them out my window as I drove off, still thinking it was only a matter of time before I was him for real, whoever they meant this time. I used to look like a lot of people, I guess.

But before long, and for all the usual reasons—afternoons in the sun, long nights out—no one could even squint me into the boy next door anymore. I was just some guy. You know the kind of non-character I'm talking about: irritable, doughy, sexless. A night manager or desk clerk. I read for parts in movies with apes and dogs in them, or talking babies and dogs or baby spies. I'd get there early, do some funny yelling, make faces, strain my voice. They never called me back and I didn't blame them. A man can get so down on his luck that he can't play anything but. I quit the business and settled into the role of some guy in real life.

Which is one thing. But, like I said, no one would even believe me when I told them I almost made it. They'd *yeah-right* me and *sure-thing-Vince* me every time. *Whatever you say, man.* "No, man," I'd go, pointing at the TV from my barstool, my shirt riding up, exposing half my butt. "They called me back. Twice!" Then they'd imitate me squeakily, or sneak their drinks onto my tab, or make fun of the lemon pie I made for my birthday.

Eventually, I found some new bars, and talked about the news instead of my hard luck. Whenever they changed the subject to women, I'd just laugh. What could I add? My one-night stands were like low-budget shorts, shot and screened out of sequence. One minute it'd be just me and my drink, the next I'd be on a roof . . . downtown? I'd wake up sandy, for some reason. The next time I saw her, whoever her was, she'd give me a vague look, and I'd try to return it.

Then I thought, hey, why not? By now—at some point between Pee-wee and Woody; or maybe the Bobbitts and OJ?—Judge had been out of the public eye long enough that he seemed like fair game and, well . . . like I said. So I switched to straights, crinkled my eyes, worked on my smirk. Pretty soon I had him down.

I only meant to get free drinks, maybe lunch. I'd nod up at the bar set, playing *Stripes* or *Gremlins* on afternoon cable, do that thing with my eyebrows, and get ready for the double-take. (I'd check the TV listings in advance, ask the bartender to change the channel before it came on, pretend to watch whatever, nurse my second drink.) A couple hundred bucks' worth of well pours every year was well worth a drunken *Doesn't anyone fucking knock anymore?* or an ironic *You're a single, successful guy* or two. Or *Man, you got topless-kissed by Phoebe Cates!* Then, *How many takes?* Or *Did you really whip it out in the bathroom?* It had been a closed set for those scenes, but I'd seen and heard enough over the years to tell them what they wanted to hear. Me being there, with them—in that shithole on Rosecrans at two o'clock in the afternoon on Tuesday—told them what not to ask. And soon enough they'd be on to Phoebe anyway, and talk about those eyes of hers and that mouth some, and how she looked great wet—how that's some kind of test, in fact: Does she look hot wet? *Hot girls look even hotter wet*, they'd say. Then, *What happened to her? She get fat or old or something? Did it all fall on her?*

I read somewhere where *Fast Times* rental tapes used to wear and snap at the exact same spot: right when Phoebe unhooks her top. The shops had to splice and resplice, then splice some more because over time the tapes kink and the tracking gets fucked. The image waves and jerks and freezes—a staticky mess of worn and grainy frames from all the pausing and slo-moing and frame-by-framing. All these years and Phoebe's still our fantasy. I can only imagine how she feels.

If I'm being honest, I guess I always knew that it could also work with women, too, my fake Judge. And it did. Once, and by accident, I swear. I mean, I'm not proud, but I'm not gonna lie either. We were both having a hard time, but her hard time was worse. I tell myself we would've hooked up anyway, and maybe we would've. She came up to me.

But what do I know? With me, it always felt like an accident. Nothing was ever anyone's fault. I only know this time was different, that Alix was different.

Say her name with a couple of *e*'s in the middle and an *x* that sounds like *s*, then a silent *e*. She told me she was from Rhode Island—someplace I knew only from maps and jokes—and that she didn't know where she was headed. Alaska, maybe. Idaho?

Alix had a birthmark on her right hip in the shape of the *s*-sounding *x*, and she said that even though that's how she got her name, it now meant more than that—the *x*—namely, her self-imposed exile from home. But also her soul, which had always been silently searching for a spot to mark. She told me this at the bar, but that's not how our conversation started. It started with her putting a can of housepaint on the seat next to mine and saying, "I feel like I know you from somewhere."

"I'm Judge Reinhold," I said, not really thinking but also thinking that was what she wanted to hear. She laughed. And I winked. I couldn't help myself.

"I'm Alix," she said, and I pictured it with different letters. Then she told me she had no bra on. She picked her breasts up and let them go to show me, and I watched them rise and fall as best I could beneath her flannel.

"Gonna do some painting?" I said, nodding at the can of paint.

"Found it in the parking lot," she said. Then she undid her belt to show me the birthmark. It looked smooth, her hip.

"Let's get out of here," I said, and just like that, we did. It felt like old times. Easy.

On the other hip, it turned out, was a constellation of freckles and moles in the rough shape of a star. I bit her ass like an apple and she said yes.

The next morning, I got up before her to take a piss, and saw her wallet next to the sink. I went through it, not to find out her first name, but to learn her last. She didn't have any ID, but she did have a hunting license in the name of some dude and a tiny laminated black-and-white drawing of a house on a rock in a bay.

"Who's the hunter?" I asked, back in bed, not thinking how weird a question it was, but for whatever reason—maybe even the same reason: being distracted and abstracted by loss—she didn't think it was weird.

"My ex," she said. And she went on to tell me how she had just left him for good, just like how his old man had up and split, too. And then how, growing up, kids used to call her ex Caspar and faggot and how he would call her rich girl, even though they were both broke. And once, in bed, he told her, "I wish you had a tiny dick and would fuck me with it."

"But I don't know why I'm talking about my ex all of a sudden," she said. Then she told me how, when she was a kid, she used to hear *all of a sudden* like some guy's name—Oliver Sudden. She thought he was this creep who'd just show up when you least expected or wanted, like in a folktale: a tricky little middle-of-the-night dickhead like Rumpelstiltskin or Jack Frost. "Jesus," she said, "why can't I stop talking."

I slid down and looked up at her as if to say *I'm here to help*, and parted the nappy terrycloth curtain of the robe she had borrowed on her way to the can, and I couldn't get it up, so I ate her pussy with as much gusto as my well-whiskey belly would allow, which wasn't much, I'm afraid. But she tasted clean, like rain on steel. "That was intimate," she said afterward. Then I told her I'd gone through her wallet in the bathroom. She lay beside me, her robe open and her downy lady fuzz goldening in the morning light.

"And I'm not Judge Reinhold," I said. "I'm just some guy."

"I wasn't expecting much," she said, "but you seem like someone."

"I'm Vince Vincent."

"See? You're honest."

"I told you I was someone I'm not," I said.

"I didn't believe you. Besides, no one's who they say they are," she said, adding that if you looked up Rhode Island in the 1987 *Encyclopædia Britannica* you would find the same drawing of that house from her wallet. It was where she spent her summers, growing up, and this was reason enough to leave home. "But I drank from the fountain," she said.

I had no idea what she meant, but even so, it got to me because it sounded sad and she looked sad when she said it, so I told her my old man used to laminate all kinds of things—report cards, ticket stubs, fall leaves. Then I tried once more to get inside her, and again it didn't work so well, and when I gave up she looked away, walked her fingers through my hair, scratching my scalp like we'd known each other longer. It felt nice. Intimate, like she said. She told me that her ex had just OD'd. They had broken up, a while back, and he had backslid. She told me she'd kissed his dead forehead four days ago in a morgue and it had felt like marble against her lips. "But that's just how dead skin feels against your lips," she said. "It's something I know. Something I already knew, I mean. I knew it then."

Because this was the second ex she'd lost that month. They died two weeks apart.

"Oh," I said. "Wow."

"Wow?"

"I mean. How are you?"

She laughed and stopped. "I cry all the time," she said, then did, just like that.

I didn't know what to do. "Is there anything I can do?" I asked.

She looked down at my crotch, which looked like napping puppies. "Apparently not," she said.

"Oh."

"I'm sort of kidding."

"Ha," I said.

She snorted her tears. "It's not about me. I just want to think about something else. I want to move my body forward through time and space."

"Like a car," I said, disliking myself.

"I can't even say his name without falling apart. I've lost two people. Everything happens twice. I want to forget and I want to remember. You know, Vince? You look more like a Judge to me."

"I should've been."

"What are you trying to say?"

"I was supposed to have his career. I should have got that part. I wouldn't have wound up like this," I said, gesturing at my apartment with my free hand—and maybe accidentally including her in my gesture.

She pulled her arm out from under my back and got out of bed. "Lying to me is one thing," she said. She let my robe fall to the floor, stood nude for a moment above me in its dirty terrycloth pool, then stepped out of it and into her jeans and shirt. "But lying to yourself will fuck you up," she said. She grabbed her wallet but left the can of paint.

If I ever see Alix again I'll tell her sorry—tell her that I am sorry—even though she likely won't remember me or care. I promise this to myself whenever I remember her, which these days is more and more. That essy *x* haunts me still. Same with those two dead exes in as many weeks. And her lighting out for wherever. That's how our movies used to end, with the hero leaving home, lighting out for the territories. Now he returns, like in Europe or Iran. Our lives no longer form long, steady arcs that go someplace else—they jerk back and forth and back again; they freeze and fail to track.

But maybe she'll watch *Fast Times* and remember. You can see where they cut me out, if you look for it. Somewhere in between Brad getting fired from All-American Burger and quitting Captain Hook's.

On my last night in L.A., I was biking home when I turned the corner at Pico onto Vermont and everything got cool and dark and quiet, the way it will in places where no one wants to live under anyone else and wants a yard or at least a driveway.

Farther down the block a car crept alongside a young woman who walked with her head down and her arms wrapped around her chest. Meaty dudes inside the car smacked their lips and talked at her. I pedaled faster and wedged my bike between her and the car.

"Why so cold, baby, why so cold—"

"Leave her alone," I said.

"What's your deal, man!"

"Leave her alone, right now," I said more loudly, and took a deep, cheap-seats breath.

"No you should—"

"You should leave alone girls out alone at night," I yelled, and brought my fist down on the roof of the car, denting it half as deep as my fist, and again just as deep, and a third time twice as deep, bringing the headliner down onto the fat ball-capped head of the talking fucking talker.

"Dude, what the *fuck*—"

"I WILL PUKE YOU!"

"Drive!" someone inside said, and they sped off to cruise Wilshire or Hollywood, or head back to Eagle Rock. Probably I was more trouble than she was worth to them. Turns out we do still do math after high school after all.

"Are you okay?" I asked the woman, mellow as possible, which wasn't as mellow as I would've liked. I only have a voice for mics and sound booths, not stages or streets. It gets a little tight when I need to be heard under imperfect conditions. My face was doing what it's always doing, which is nothing. My face had frozen like that a while back.

She kept walking, head down, boot heels clicking concrete. I coasted beside her, my gears spinning.

"Are you all right?"

No answer, just *click, click, click, click.*

"Those guys were pricks."

She walked faster, and I quit coasting and started pedaling again.

"My name is Vince."

Nothing.

"You don't know me from anywhere."

But she had turned sharply down an alley, and I didn't follow. I didn't want to scare her any more than she already was. I braked and watched her disappear down the alley. It lit up with security lights as she walked.

When I got to my apartment, I pried open Alix's paint can with six take-out chopsticks and dumped it all into my plugged-up tub. It looked thick and blue. "Look how blue," I said, realizing how quiet it was. "Hello!" I said, a little louder. I opened the blinds and took off my shoes and socks and pants and shirt and stepped into the paint. My feet were in, then my balls were in, the backs of my knees. I rolled over and coated my front. I got out and walked, bluely dripping, to the living room, took a breath, and ran toward the far wall full bore, smacking painted junk and belly against the cool white, leaving behind a blue smear of fat blue gut and nuts: a thickly splattered middle-of-a-man shape. Then, beneath it, with a wet blue finger, I wrote "I WAS HERE" for my landlord or super to find when I finally broke my lease and lit out for somewhere a little closer to home.

(...etc....)

Clay Blackall III

Is this you?: I like to see where I'm going, and am not alone in this. Or so an especially kindly intake shrink once assured me. As a child I refused to enter submarines and Ground Rounds* alike.

> *Est. 1969, a date of which they are now Pround. Back in my day, the regional restaurant chain was a kind of proto-Applebee's or Chuck E. Cheese's, albeit with neither the colonized appetizers of the former nor the latter's redemption games and anthropomorphic hosts. Instead Ground Round screened Cat v. Mouse cartoons and not only allowed but encouraged its preteen party guests to discard their spent peanut shells directly onto the floor. Eli's last birthday party* was held at their North Main location, across from the hole that used to be Sears.
>
> > *At his fifth, our old man had thrown a knife into the kiddie pool, so next year Eli got to pick the spot. Eli also chose the invitations, which pictured Harold Lloyd spanking a woman with her shoe. We pulled into the

Ground Round parking lot, and that's when I saw the front door. It looked like the entrance to a crypt. My jaw clenched, my knees locked, and sweat bit my eyes. Ignoring her husband's oh-for-fuck-sakes, Mother stayed behind while, in the backseat, I farted and pretended to read *The Indigestible MAD*. The car next to us tilted from the weight of old newspapers and the large man to whom they meant something. "Just think of it as a castle you've been invited to," Mother said. "For a ball!" She made a vaguely regal gesture with her hand and cracked the windows. Her sunglasses were on, and her voice was smaller than normal. The night before, she had fallen down the stairs.* "Fine," she said. "See where this gets you." I looked up from Don Martin's *Jekyll and Hyde* long enough to catch my mother asking the parking lot where she'd gone wrong, then disappearing behind that heavy wooden door.**

*It had been a long night for all of us. My father spent it playing the piano that his father still insisted he couldn't play and that his wife wished he wouldn't. At some point Mother came into my room to check on me and said, "It's okay, Clay. Your father has his garden and I have mine. We all have our own gardens."

**Next year Mother and Father would be dead, and that was that for a lot of things, but especially anniversaries.

Judge Reinhold: Pauline Kael called him "a young man with an old man's name," even though these days I'd bet he feels the other way around.

[L.A.] is neither here nor there: In Providence, where one experiences many different times at the same time, we have too much of both. Once, while walking past a downtown strip club, I caught myself thinking, I remember when that place *used* to be a strip club. Now, for the second or third time, it's a hotel again. Turns out time is neither straight nor shapeless; it is instead like coral: whorled, fragile, and made of skeletons.

Window: At every opportunity my college literature professor, Vseslav Botkin, would celebrate the humble window—"the solace of first-person literature throughout the ages." But by the time I wound up in his classroom (Fall '83), the always eccentric Dr. Botkin was like a nautilus that had lost its spiral. Upon failing to locate the first of all those numbered index cards stashed in his many jacket pockets, professor would go off book. After asking the first few rows questions they couldn't answer—such as where, for instance, the samovar sat in his childhood home, or how many dolls it took to get to the last of his *babu*'s matyroshkas—he'd proceed to upbraid the entire class. Above all else, he despised our mediocre desires, which, much to his dismay, we took to mean career goals. "Therapist? Critic!" He spat nothing and made what amounted to a fist. "These are your souls . . . Look! I crush them like ants!"

All these years and Phoebe's still our fantasy: Okay, but how about Jennifer Jason Leigh? And Molly and Lea and Ally? Though they might not have got under our skin like Ms. Cates, they still hold a special place in our hearts. Plus, the ever-touching Jennifer Jason has taken off her top in damn near every film in which she has appeared.* As for Ally, well, I wouldn't kick her out of bed for being crackers. The winter after I graduated from Brown, on the drive back from the Seekonk Showcase, Eli and I had what might have been our last argument about her *Breakfast Club* character. Eli was midway through his freshman year at my alma mater—our legacy once again causing as many problems as it solved. It was movie night for the Hafkins, and we were damned if we were going to see *The Purple Rose of Cairo* with the grandfolks. And so, on the way home, Eli and I argued about whether or not the problem was that Sheedy had presented a grotesque caricature of the high school outcast—call it dorksploitation or pizzaface—or just that she had sold out for a fucking jock, who we both knew was really Repo Man. While we bickered in the backseat, a distracted Grandpa Ike nearly hit the parking lot cop and did hit the parade barricade erected to calm Friday-night traffic. We shunpiked it home in silence, our one working headlight winking into the night. Our last movie night. And now I can't remember which sides we even took. They both sound like me. Him, too. Eli loved Ally Sheedy for real. But our agreements had more question marks and exclamation points in them than most people's arguments, so who's to say? Point being, we mostly left each other alone for a reason.

> *And then there's the matter of her actor-father getting killed for real in a remake of a TV show—a sudden, horrific, and pointless event to which I can and do relate. From *Flesh & Blood* on, Jennifer Jason Leigh burns through the screen, trying with all her might to make it all mean something real, this make-believe life into which she was born. We could soothe each other, Jennifer—Jen? Jenn? Surely not Jenny . . . JJ?—and mumble our troubles into each other's ears. I lost my dad, too, you know, and my mother. Brother, also. My sister has never liked me. You could pretend it was all a movie. *Jennifer.*

Rhode Island: I've long held that the motto of our Union's smallest, most densely populated state should be "Small But Dense." But up until twelve I thought Connecticut was the

Construction State and that Vagina Is for Lovers.* I also thought that Providence was Washington, D.C., and that Nixon lived in the State House, which I thought was our nation's Capitol Building, which I thought was the White House.** The Internet-savvy reader, meanwhile, knows Rhode Island only as the most difficult state upon which to click.

*I'd also always read Episcopal as *Epi-social*, which, like most of the mistakes you make as a kid, makes a lot of sense in retrospect, like wearing a *milestone* around your neck or ending something in one *fail* swoop. I also used to think that we call it Indian giving because white men "gave" the Indians land that had already belonged to them, then took it back again. What else could it mean?

**A common mistake, I'd imagine, given all the shared white marble clichés and despite the State House's window A/C units. But to further confuse matters, my father's genitals, on frequent household display—Pa made the creaky morning trek from master bedroom to toilet in a threadbare and barely hiked-down wife-beater—looked, to my brother and me, an awful lot like our thirty-seventh president:

My Old Man's Dick

Richard Milhous Nixon

Only knew from . . . jokes: Now that I think of it, maybe our motto should be "The Punch Line State." Two that have stuck with me:

> *"G-U-N-P-O-W-D-E-R spells tobacco . . . and B-A-T, Rhode Island!"*

And:

> *"It's a terribly . . . tiny little country. Rhode Island could beat the crap out of it in a war."*

Encyclopædia Britannica: This is sure enough what happens to Rhode Islanders fixing to split and/or reinvent themselves. On your way out the door, your childhood home—the place where your cherry got popped or you chopped down your old man's cherry tree or shot your first load or goose—becomes a local landmark. We all feel like museum pieces round these parts.

Drank from the fountain: Built in 1873, the carved marble and granite drinking fountain sits at the foot of the front steps of the Providence Athenaeum. The water—rich in cadmium, mercury, and sundry pathogens—flows straight from the Pawtuxet River. The inscription carved above its spigot reads "Come Hither Whoever Thirsteth."* According to local legend, whoever follows this advice will be doomed to return to and eventually die in Providence. Anecdotal evidence seems to bear this out, at least among members of my and my parents' generation. I've managed to avoid the fountain's lure, though Eli—who would fill his thermos at it on his way to work—declared the water oddly cool and clean and sweet. Many of Providence's finest succumbed. Over and over, again and again, they'll try to pull up their roots, but every other fall or spring or summer will find themselves moving back. To make a little cash, maybe, or to sublet something cheap from an undergrad, or to house- and cat-sit for a restless professor until they get over a breakup, or kill a little time with an old flame, or finally finish that book they've been working on or reading. The fountain often takes the blame. The hapless prefer to think of themselves as helpless.

> *None other than Howard Phillips Lovecraft wet his whistle here, despite an inborn fear of germs and the outdoors. But the local horror writer and racist was afraid of everyone and everything you'd care to name: people unlike himself, himself, the sea. What else? Women, it almost goes without saying. New York. Genitals. "The oldest and strongest emotion of mankind is fear," our boy once wrote. "And the oldest and strongest kind of fear is fear of the unknown."

She told me that her ex had just OD'd: Alix, Eli's favorite student and last ex, was also the last ex of his former cellmate, sometime coworker, and maybe even friend, Rob Nolan (*see my notes to Twinrock Caretaker's Log*), whose corpse she here describes.

I am sorry: During his commencement week Eli stopped by my office* to tell me that he had just the night before apologized to a blonde with kind, close-set eyes whom he'd never even met, let alone fucked in the reeds outside Swan Point the weekend prior like he'd thought. And yet, a mere twenty minutes later he was fingering this wrong girl in a dormitory rec room while they watched that show where an unglamorous man leaps from one historic site to the next. He'd already gotten the apology out of the way upfront, so after she came she happily quid-pro-quo'd him off into a slop sink in the custodial closet just off the rec room. "That was fun," she said afterward, smiling a Cornhusker or Sooner smile. "You're really *interesting*. I don't usually meet interesting guys like you." Then she told him that as a freshman she had accidentally pricked herself with a needle full of DNA degerminator and that it was erasing her code as they spoke. No one knew exactly what would happen to her, but she would almost certainly die young. Eli watched her swallow and heard the loudest nothing. Then she took him up to her room to show him a realistic acrylic of return pipes she had painted the previous semester. Or was it Victorian tampon packaging? Either way, Eli pretended to have something in his eye—Dryer lint? Asbestos? They had been in a basement—and told her he was leaving for Turkey in the morning. Afterward, he huffed tape head cleaner from his roommate's Cookie Monster. It was, he assured me, a dark high.

"Christ, just how *many* women have you been with?" I asked him.

He leaned back in his chair and banged his head against the wall three times. "You suck the life out of me," he said.

"But you wind up with the goddamnedest-looking girls," I said. "Do you have any pictures?"

He said, "I'm changing my name to Hafkin,"** and left.

*My short-lived public notary business. That there was no money to be made in simply witnessing things was beside the point. I figured if I played my cards right—starchy meals in, and apartments in neighborhoods where children had no bedtimes—I could make a go of it. And failing that, I could call my office home, which is exactly what I did once the state revoked my license.

**City Hall was right down the street—take a left at the plaque indicating the high-water mark from the Hurricane of '38.

Home: Our shared fetish. Look at the gingerbread house upon which I now nibble, for example. The Jew in me can't abide sitting and watching food harden into tchochkes. At the same time my

WASP half, well accustomed to diminishing generational returns, can't quite bring itself to defile this symbol of bygone festivity, home/hearth, and seasonable weather. Hence my guilty little strikes with a Swiss Army knife purchased countless Januaries ago with three Hanukkahs' worth of gelt. It's almost denuded of edible bits—the house. Even the front door, a graham cracker, is gone. A stale Kiss or two is all that's left. But I can always just lick the windows, which appear to have been made from melted-down Life Savers. I'm peering in right now.

Twinrock Caretaker's Log
Jamestown, Rhode Island

Rob Nolan

Winter 2000–2001

11/6/00

Flushed and scrubbed cistern.

Replaced escutcheon plate on master bedroom door.

Recaulked kitchen sink.

Stacked and sorted firewood.

Snuck some rainwater. Tastes fine to me.

Will dry and split punked logs for kindling.

11/7/00

Stained lee-facing wainscoting. I'm not sure how many more winters it has left in it. Should probably get replaced this fall or next.

Bulgur sack full of moth larvae. But the rainwater stayed down.

11/8/00

Sanded deck.

11/9/00

Reset interior cladding beneath SE bay window.

Went ashore to get a fresh sack of grain and make a call.

11/12/00

Replaced brass doorknobs with black porcelain ones as requested.

Ended up using only twenty of them. Some were too cracked or bent. Where'd you get these? I'm guessing an abandoned Fall River Victorian. New Bedford? Nice find. I spent a lot of time in burnt houses as a kid. Vacant lots, too. Central Falls had its share of both.

11/15/00

Cleared dead gulls and gull parts from roof turbine. Bleached doorknobs.

If you had any idea what goes on in vacant houses in places like New Bedford, you might rethink the scavenger approach. It doesn't bother me, but rich folks spook easy.

11/17/00

Replaced basement sewage line.

Water rats in the cellar. Will club and drown them tomorrow.

11/18/00

Clubbed and drowned rats.

Used a burlap sack from the root cellar. Will replace it when I go ashore to try and call X again. She's home. She just won't pick up. I know her hours. Might take tomorrow off to drive up to Providence. Stop by her work. Can't stand loose ends. I mean, I'll peel labels off beers and unravel rope, but I try to leave things looking better than when I found them.

Weighed down the sack with rusted peach cans. Figured they wouldn't be missed.

11/19/00

11/20/00

Shit, I can write what I want. You won't read this, Fud. X used to always say I was paranoid. I'll show her. There's all kinds of things you don't care about, I bet. Least of all me. Besides, I can always just burn it.

And now here I am, talking to you, thinking of her. Neither of you are here. You could be, though. You could pour yourself a drink, watch the sun set past the bridge, and spend a late fall night by the fire, with all that water beating against this rock and the shore and rocking all the empty boats anchored side by each and falling and rising with the tide, and there's a bell and some far-off human noise I can't name or shake that might be traffic or just my ears ringing, and all these empty rooms. The sea smells more like itself the darker the sky gets, and it makes me think how some people close their eyes when they eat what they love. I used to make fun of people like that. Look at you, I'd say or think, with your chocolate or your cheese. Just like in ads. Like it's heroin. Oh what bliss. It almost hurts. But we don't smell the sea, we smell what it's washed up. I close my eyes, turn off the lights. You should be here.

11/21/00

Cleaned all 65 windows. Spent the evening clearing the dried-out quick from my nails with the last razor blade. The blood doesn't come no matter how deep I dig, like I'm all skin. I keep digging.

11/22/00

Will replace the windows I broke—six in all, counting the attic portholes. Those will be a bitch. Means another trip to Providence, but that's my fault. Luckily I still know some glass guys. Painters drink beer and smoke grass, like to hang out. Glaziers like the harder stuff and run in tighter circles. They were okay after work. I used to know this one guy, Mikey, at Brown Plant Ops. Dude had a face like a smoke-shop Indian but wore rolled-up clamdiggers and little white espadrilles. He also called men by their hair colors. "Check out this brunette," he'd say. We called Mikey the manly faggot. Whenever he was on a jag, he liked to melt his coke in warmed-up whiskey and swig at it from an ass pocket all shift long. I used to think he was a little rough with the glass, but it turned out that gritty sound was just him grinding his teeth. At least once a year Mikey takes what he calls "vacations" at a local nuthouse, and Brown picks up the tab.

I'd try to get a job like his, but I work alone. Besides, they'd probably feed me some bullshit about preexisting conditions, when my whole life is a preexisting condition. Or just not hire me. There are some gaps in my history that are hard to explain without bringing up all kinds of crap that won't help. That's why I like working for old guys like you. You wouldn't even know what to ask. Institutions and HR folks are on top of that shit, though. Unlike most people, I have no desire to be where I'm not wanted. You need to ask me in.

Will call to arrange the glass before heading up. Maybe I'll try X again while I'm at it.

11/23/00

Replaced and reglazed all six windows.

Will clean putty residue off glass tomorrow. Need Windex, newspaper, razor blades. This olden-days rag and vinegar crap from the handbook just won't cut it. Look, I've stolen drugs from homeless women and used works off stiffs. Set fields on fire. Poked a kid's eye out with a stick. The French have a word that means someone missing an eye. When I asked a French girl I used to shack with why they even need the word, she said, "But how else would you know how to call them?" and looked at me like I was crazy or stupid. Sometimes I think I should've been born European.

11/24/00

I don't understand why X won't just give it to me straight. I know she fucked that line cook who acts like he never knows my name. I can see it when I close my eyes and try to sleep. Fucking dreadlock prick—don't you point your chin at *me*. That's not how to say *hey*. But I want her to admit it to my face. I want to see her mouth when she owns up to all of it. She winced when she said we were through, and that hurt. Like I would ever hit her. Jesus. Even if I could see nothing but my own face in her eyes, I wouldn't so much as raise a hand. When you grow up like I did, you either hit your woman all the fucking time or not at all. Maybe once. So I just looked at her, then looked away and slowly pressed my fist into the wall until it cracked, then quick threw some things into a hockey bag—a clean set of shirts, a fistful of pens, a couple blank books X couldn't sell due to bloodstains. Meanwhile, I lost count at nine of how many times out on the curb Georgie Carwash said fuck per minute.

11/25/00

Pumped out and mopped cellar.

It occurs to me that you can't know who Georgie Carwash is. That's something rich girls do that drives me nuts—mention strangers in passing like you must know who the fuck they're talking about. Like they're four years old and you couldn't possibly not know the name of their new best friend or pretend horsey or monster in the closet. So, just so you know, Georgie Carwash is this two-bit gangster with dickholes for eyes that spends the day leaning on a mop in front of the club across Carpenter Street from our apartment. (Just like me to use *our*, now that I can't. Man, those *your*'s and *my*'s sure caused some fights. *My place, your place*—either way was trouble.)

But *club* makes it sound nice: this place is a grim little shack for tracksuit goons to enjoy loose talk and poker and whatever they drink. No windows. And out front, Georgie paces the sidewalk, yelling at hookers, chatting up what few cute girls walk by unescorted, and washing bottom-rung hoods' Lincolns—which is how he got the name. His *shits* and *fucks* and *motherfuckers* were the first thing we heard in the morning and the last we heard at night. The Tourette's rooster, X calls him. *Cocksucker-Motherfucker-Doodle-Doo!* The cursing got under X's skin from the start, but I got a kick out of it, at least at first. It got old quick.

Anyway, I had always meant to add up a minute's worth of Georgie's fucks, and last Tuesday morning looked like my last chance, even though I had other things on my mind at the time, like X telling me if I so much as looked her up when I got back, she'd call the cops, which is no joke for an ex-con, and she knows it. So sure enough, I lost count of Georgie's curses somewhere around the forty-second mark and was too wound up to give it another shot.

It's not that I think I'm any better than anyone else, because I'm not: we're all pieces of shit in one way or another—just fucking pick a reason. No, it's just that maybe if I set my mind to it, I might be able to straighten a few things out and maybe even save somebody from someone other than myself for a change.

12/01/00

Three weeks into our breakup and you can see the right-hand L-O-V-E tattoo again through all the scars. That's the hand I used to run through her hair. Her hair smelled like the wind. Like lightning. Like something most people don't even know has a smell but does.

Varnished deck.

12/24/00

Oiled screen doors, weather vane. Took down fucking chimes.

1/2/01

Went to pick up Naval Jelly at the Quaker Lane Lowe's and just kept driving north. Caught some traffic in Cranston, so it was dark by the time I hit the city. Went to the bar down the street from our apartment, grabbed a stool by the window, drank six club sodas with lime, gnawed at the rinds like an alcoholic, and waited for our kitchen light to come on, on the lookout for two shadows behind the curtains I bought from an antique dealer for her twenty-ninth birthday. But the lights never came on, which could mean any number of things. In the end, I'm betting none of us got any sleep.

1/5/01

Oiled cabinets.

Sometimes I want to eat myself.

1/6/01

Our breakup fight was over neither of us being able to make a right fist: her from hand-stitching blank books I knew no one would buy, and me from punching walls, mirrors, my own skull. She didn't want to hear about her choices, and before long we had both said some things and I made it a point to leave it at that. Like I said: I won't hit a girl no matter what. But they've hit me plenty. At least the ones with balls. I still have scars from Viv. She would claw me like a cat when she was pissed, which was often. Poor Yvette would just ball her tiny fists under my chin and burst into tears. My jaw still clicks when I yawn from the one time X coldcocked me. I almost always have it coming. But she shouldn't work with her hands and have two and a half jobs. She could go out and get one perfectly normal desk job anytime she wanted. That was my whole fucking point. My mom had no choice in life, and it killed her. It makes me want to punch something.

Our fight went like this: "So who are you now?"

"I only want . . ." she started.

"What!" I got close. "What do you *want*?"

"People to love me. I want people to love me."

I waited for her to cry, and when she didn't, I said, "There you go."

"You don't know. When I was a girl . . ." She stopped herself.

I tried to smirk, but couldn't. She could probably tell I didn't know what to do with my face.

"You're still a girl," I said finally, and closed the door behind me as quietly as I could.

1/7/01

X's hair's still black, but she doesn't plait it into two braids anymore. Now she wears it up, with stray strands hanging here and there, down and around her neck. I used to hold that neck. She looks rested, though, so good for her. I miss those braids. I won't call them pigtails—that's an ugly name for something beautiful. Like cunt. Or bird. Gorge. You can tell a lot by the names we give things. This world is wasted on us. I've never owned much, but I've lost things same as anyone. We've broken up more times than I can count. But she tells me this is it.

I sleep in the turret and can hear the turbine spinning this way, then pausing, ticking twice, then a longer pause and back that way. Last night I picked up the cot and brought it downstairs. The creaks are fine, it's the tick-tick that gets to me. Will rig up some kind of lock in the morning.

1/11/01

Made turbine brake out of coat hanger hooks and sisal.

You know X, but I'm not going to tell who she is, even though it would hurt you if I did. I want to hurt you. But X—I've done enough.

1/23/01

Went ashore to buy bread and hot dogs. I think my mom was a good mom even though I turned nine before ever eating a hot hot dog and twice a week had to help her up the front steps and into bed and even more than that near the end. I thought the name was ironic, like a fat guy called Slim, or calling the mayor Your Honor, because I only ate them cold out of my fist, like breadsticks, and used to lick the salt off my fingers until my mom's old man smacked me. He made me call him Pop. I could tell you exactly what Pop said when he smacked me, but I won't. Sometimes it feels like not repeating him is the only power I have.

Only enough matches for a fireplace fire and restarting it, so for supper I roasted my hot dog on a stick. Saving the bread for tomorrow.

1/27/01

My mom was young when she had me and when she died. To go with the breast cancer she'd already had, she got brain cancer from the sewing machine she hung her head over forty-eight hours a week for at least a thousand weeks. Electromagnetic fields. I would watch her change. I remember wondering, Did they get thrown out or put in a jar or burned in a furnace? I looked to Pop's bookshelf for answers, and all I found was a book on World War II, which I hid in my room. I'd read it under the covers with a flashlight. It was the piles of bodies that made me feel most ashamed. But I couldn't stop myself from looking night after night. The pictures made me feel weak in a way I liked. I felt delicate, like paper.

I missed two pantry shifts at the restaurant to bury her. I asked for more time off, and my boss told me, "We all got folks who die," and went back to sweating onions. "Life is showing up," he added over his shoulder. Later, during one of his six smoke breaks, I pissed in the chicken stock, took his knives, and walked out the front door through the dining room. At home I tattooed L-O-V-E on the knuckles of my left hand and was about to write H-A-T-E on the right when I realized I needed all the help I could get and went with L-O-V-E again. Come on, world, I thought. I'm right here.

"Tell him I died," my dad supposedly instructed my mom right before he split. I wasn't even born yet. "I was young," my mom told me when I turned nine and started asking questions. "But he had these white jeans and looked like Steve McQueen."

"Hank LaChance was a chucklehead," yelled Pop from the parlor. "Ham-and-egging son of a bitch cost us the States. Twice!" Pop couldn't see worth a damn, but he had ears like a bat. He kicked my father off his coaching staff *before* he knocked up my mom, who at that point had been going out with his starting center. I'm glad Mom at least had a little fun at one point.

She was seventeen when she met my old man, who was twenty-nine. Thirty? Who knows. Older than her. I watched the second hand sweep across the face of the kitchen clock. "Sex makes kids," my mom whispered at me after it had swept past the 3456789. "Don't forget that. You'll save trouble."

Me, I've always liked older women. They've got more of whatever it is that makes us different from the animals we wear and eat and keep as pets, and they at least know to lick their goddamn finger before they go sticking it where they shouldn't. But I'm talking about college girls when I mean young. A high schooler? Come on. I'd rather fuck a sack of cats and knuckles. But my mom was old inside, like me, and for a lot of the same reasons. Who knows about my old man. I sure don't.

Cleaned all the cloudy mirrors with alcohol and covered them with sheets. To keep them clean.

2/12/01

When this job is through, I'll need a place of my own. I'm thinking of moving back to the East Side, where all the trees are and X isn't, and where they don't have house fires, except for that one time my painting crew forgot to hose down the side we had just heat-stripped. It burst into flames while we were fifteen minutes into cold beers at the Hot Club, watching the sun set over the power plant. When we saw the smoke rising from College Hill, we even joked about it. It was a Friday. No one got hurt, but our boss got sued and we got fired.

I'm sorry I didn't see it up close. Watching it burn might have really been something.

When I was twelve, I set that one field on fire but didn't have the guts to watch. It wasn't an accident, but I could've easily pretended it was. Back then, people might've believed me. If I knew then what I know now—that getting in trouble is just a bunch of bullshit they use to keep you in line—I would've stuck around to see the flames eat the grass in lines and feel that hot nothing inside me, somewhere up above my balls, until my knees shook.

Real trouble's not something you get into or out of. It's something you are or are not.

Weather was warm. Recemented loose steps. Four in all.

2/13/01

The last time I lived on the East Side was in the early '90s, in a Mount Hope four-bedroom with drop ceilings and roommates who would fake break-ins to steal and hock each other's shit, then pool money to buy it back. Near the end, when we hadn't paid rent for at least two months, our landlord, Ike Hafkin, sent his kid over to block their van in the driveway with a long black Skylark. He got out, sniffed at no one, pulled up his jeans, and walked away, smiling. Later, we slim-jimmed his Buick, pushed it down the street, drove the van to a friend's, then pushed the car back and locked it up. When the kid returned the next day and saw the van gone but the car exactly where he had left it, he looked to the right, to the left, then up at the sky. I watched between the blinds, from the couch.

I never liked that kid or his slumlord dad, but him crying on the sidewalk has stuck with me just the same. Then he put something from his pocket into his mouth, and I went to go throw up. I tend not to think, Poor kid, about any kind of rich kid, let alone some crybaby who's older than me, but he sure looked like there'd be hell to pay when he got home, and I can feel that.

I came out of my nod to see my worst roommate, Zeke, nodding, across from me. Wet? I thought. Wet. At his feet, an empty bucket. "Fuck?" I asked, and threw the first thing I found at him. He flickered awake. "Fuck," I said.

"You weren't breathing," he said.

"That's not help."

"I waited to fix."

I gave him the finger. Again, apparently.

"That's how I knew you were okay," he said.

When I came out of it, it was dark and quiet and Zeke was gone.

At the end of the month, Hafkin evicted us. We scattered, and I wound up downtown, I think, over a gay bar for poor gays—twenty bucks a week, week to week.

I got clean, met Cliff and all those noise dudes. Then Cliff got the idea to live in a mill building above a flea market. Things were looking up.

2/14/01

Maybe I could pull off a place on Ives or Governor, at the wrong end of Fox Point. Soon all that'll be left for folks like me will be Pawtucket, and after that, it's back to Central Falls. But Pawtucket's it for me. Third move's as good as a fire, Mikey used to say.

2/16/01

Unscrewed clogged sink drains, cleaned out wads of hair, scum, something that shrank in the light.

It's a small state. I could track down my old man and ask *what gives?* This is, after all, the same guy who returned again and again to the scene of the crime: who coached the same team he had let down as a player, who knocked up the high school sweetheart he missed the first time around. I can't imagine he left town. But why should I. He didn't want a kid, so he split. He was still pretty young. What man can't understand that? I can understand that. Besides, how I grew up was as much Pop's fault as it was my old man's. I've made all my own choices in this life. It's pretty easy to understand what's what if you're being honest.

2/27/01

I wound up doing time for some straight-up wrong-place/wrong-time-type bullshit. Look, I know firsthand how it's like this with every con, and I'm not saying I am or was or ever will be innocent—no one is. But what got me put away was not my fault. This was when I was twenty-two and had been using on and off, mostly on, since I was eighteen, so I already had my share of chickenshit priors—copping, holding, breaking & entering—but I'm not going to talk about junk. People will go on and on about it, but in the end it's pretty fucking simple: first it makes you feel great, then good, then only okay, then back and forth between that and shit till you finally decide to kick and go through hell and back just to get to a whole new kind of dull. Make no mistake: in the long run, shit is awful. But in the short run? Well . . . There you are.

This particular story starts with me chasing down a girl named Viv, who wasn't a junkie yet and who wouldn't finish art school and looked great knocking in bank shots and back shots of rum. At some point her rich family cut her off for skipping class and shooting up, so hocking her ex-roommate's stereo had been her idea—besides, she told me it was hers, the stereo. Seemed like a plan. Viv waited in the car and split as soon as the cops pulled up to the pawnshop. I never told them about her and did the time just like I thought a good guy would, and she never so much as came and visited. Plus she leaped at the chance to get clean without me around to drag her down—at a fancy retreat in Newport, and on her folks' dime. This was when I was young and still wanted the kind of woman that got painted on the sides of bombers, and not the kind bombardiers carried around pictures of: girls who kissed soft and cooled pies on windowsills. The kind of girl who'd've stuck by me.

Viv and I met at a Bad Brains show at the old Livingroom. Me and a pal split a couple bottles of Hong Kong cough syrup waiting for doors. The sunlight hurt my eyes, but I still caught hers across the parking lot. I can't remember who smiled first, but at some point we were both smiling. Later, in the pit, the codeine wore off and the ephedrine kicked in, and my vision became a smaller and smaller box, like an old, just-switched-off TV, and there she was, handing me the cherry Coke it turned out I needed all of. The color came back like that. My lungs held all the air in the club. We made out. I could taste the back of her throat and wanted more.

She was a year older, and over the next couple weeks we explored the seedier parts of Providence while we both cut class: me from Central Falls High, her from RISD. Look at you, I would say, corrupting a minor, and she would laugh. We had the same interests: punk rock and getting high. I took the bus to Providence and we'd meet up downtown, which was even more of a wasteland back then. The river was low and mostly paved over, the walking mall chockablock with wig and kung fu shops and pigeons and shitass drunks. After we had scored and fixed at this one biker bar underneath the highway, we'd sometimes split a hot dog—or a lobster roll if we were feeling rich—and a side of kidney beans at Haven Brothers. Or maybe just grab a cup of gray coffee and pocket a couple packs of crackers for later. Then we'd walk along the buried river, find the open spots, and stare down into the dark, metallic water. The river was slow and green and foul, and at low tide you could see all the rotten tires and rusted axles and whatnot sticking out of the muck.

Went up on roof. Replaced missing and broken pigeon spikes with filed-down date nails.

3/01/01

I'll give X this, she's made a point not to ask her family for money. Nothing's worse than a rich kid who acts broke. Whenever these assholes go fake broke, they just ask their folks to write them a check. Real broke is your folks hitting *you* up for cash. Rich kids like to sit back and window-shop, play it cool—confident that things will work out for them in the end. And they will. Meanwhile, guys like me, we see something we want, we know we have to take it.

So why do I keep winding up with rich girls? I don't know. I do know you can't fuck guilt away.

Punch list is filled. Will find more chores. I walk around looking for them.

3/06/01

Descaled brass faucets.

I wish I were simple enough to find pride in fixing things, not because I want to feel proud, but because feeling it over working on someone else's shit would have to mean that I'm all out of shame.

When I was making ends meet with yardwork, our crew took lunch breaks around the corner from Prospect Park. Because it was late March and still winter cold, I stayed in the truck with Teach—who I met in prison, and who hooked me up with the job once he got out. Maynor, who'd had enough of both of us, sat on the tailgate and ate the tortillas his wife had made and wrapped for him in tinfoil. I knew they were still warm, because I could see the steam rising in the rearview mirror. I couldn't believe they stayed hot like that. In between bites of my peanut butter sandwich, I tried to shut out Teach's Camel and hot coffee noises. And there she was: a moon-faced little girl in a dirty shirt with missing buttons and no shoelaces, her belly poking out in the middle of a school day. She stood on the street, just down the hill from us, looking like a refugee from someplace worse than Providence. Krakow, maybe. Some shithole in Peru. But, you know, in the late '40s or something. She might as well have been in black-and-white. And she couldn't speak English. I could just tell by looking in her eyes. The same way you can tell a virgin or a racist.

I put my sandwich down on the dashboard, next to Teach's bag of weed, and got out and brushed myself off, just in case she was allergic. Moving slowly, and trying to come off as friendly-like, I approached her. When I got a respectable distance—maybe ten feet—I made up a whole form of sign language on the spot: opening my arms to suggest a neighborhood, closing them into a triangle to represent home. She stared in my direction for what felt like an hour, me frozen in a church shape with a stupid, fake, I'm-not-the-bad-kind-of-stranger look on my face. I repeated my symbols and held them. Nothing. And again. At some point my smile cracked. Just about then, for whatever reason, she turned away and walked to the tenement just down the street—a house that, so help me, I had never noticed before. Like her, it looked like it belonged in the past, back when downtown was even worse and Benefit got real slummy in spots. Sure there are still some ratty apartments here and there, but ratty in a collegiate sense. In other words, not ratty. But this was city poverty I was looking at. Too many mailboxes stuffed with former tenants' collection notices, scaly paint the color of Chinese pollution, old sheets for curtains, the odd electric candle in the window. And when the little girl got to the basement apartment door, it opened and a grandpa-old guy pulled her inside, looking straight at me with what probably wasn't even his worst look. He waited a solid minute before closing the door, just holding it and looking at me.

Back in the truck, between slurps of coffee, Teach told me he knew him, the old guy in the basement. That he was from the Ukraine and used to be a cop in Mexico. That Teach caught hepatitis cleaning his toilet in Juárez. Then something else. Teach's stories were hard to follow. They trailed off like that.

3/11/01

Last night I slept in the only bedroom I hadn't tried, thinking it might help. It didn't. The twin beds are covered with dustcloths and look like they just died. I set my cot up in the far corner. You probably have a name for this room that I wouldn't use even if I knew it.

I woke up thinking of Georgie Carwash talking at X like he does at all the other man-less neighborhood girls. All day long he lets them have it. Is my ex fair game now? Or does Dreadlocks see her home at night? I know I should want him to, but I don't. Even though I can see—as clear and slow as cocktail ice—X alone and fumbling with the front door dead bolt while, across the street, Georgie checks his pompadour in a Plymouth's side-view, wipes back a stray pubic-looking curl with one of his meat-hook thumbs. I want to bury my hands into that gasket of neck fat and wring the air from him. I want to see those puffy slits roll back into his skull. And then I want to bash that skull against the street until it comes apart like a pumpkin. Some nights I wake up choking, my heart pumping, and I'll listen to the waves lapping against this rock and try to think of nothing, a nothing that, if I'm lucky, takes the shape of a still, clean lake instead of something human. I fall back asleep, hoping this time to sleep without dreams, like a convict lucky enough to have scored some halfway decent shit.

4/3/01

Ran into X yesterday, which turned out to be a long one. Had spent the better part of the afternoon at the corner bar, keeping an eye out for Georgie, who was nowhere to be seen, which wasn't like him. Then I saw her walk by. Yelled hey, and wait up. "Hi, Rob," she said flatly.

"Where's Georgie?"

"He brought me flowers," she said. "So I spent a couple hours staring at him through the blinds and repeating 'disappear, disappear,' over and over. The next morning he was gone, and no one's seen him since."

"You're a witch," I said, and made a point to grin just in case she got me wrong.

"You don't know the first thing about me," she said back, but not at all playfully. We talked about something else after that—work or the fucking weather—but what, I can't remember. The whole time I was fixed on her jaw, noticing how strong and set it looked, wondering if her face had gotten meaner since I'd left or if she'd always looked hard and antsy like that. Or if it was just with me. I had to say something. What could I say?

"I just want you to be with someone good, okay?" I said. "Just promise me he'll be good to you."

"How dare you say that," she said. And before I could say anything—not that I had anything helpful to say—she had already turned and headed back to what had once been our place.

After three or four hours of walking around town, I crashed at Teach's. His apartment had nothing in it and he turned in early. I couldn't sleep, but not because I couldn't sleep on floors. I spent the rest of the night staring up at his ceiling and destroying with my mind the shapes it made there.

4/16/01

Sanded soffits.

Since I'm going to burn this, I might as well fill it.

Growing up, the only non-war or non-sports-related reading around the house was Pop's collection of gas station maps, which he kept in a shoebox under the bathroom sink. By fifteen I could visualize every road and campsite and pond in southern New England. Block Island seemed the most interesting, so I broke my mom's weekly cigarette twenty for change at the milk store and took a bus to Providence, where I bought a one-way ferry ticket, figuring I could get work as a busboy or dishwasher at one of the hotels or dinner halls. In my trash bag I had a change of clothes, a hand towel, a Walkman with a couple tapes: one cool—but not then—the other never cool.

When I got out there, I walked into a couple places and they all told me I'd need some kind of parental permission because of my age, plus I'd have to do something about my hair, so I said fuck it, put my stuff in a locker, and stole an unlocked five-speed to bike out to the bluffs, where I figured there'd be some good swimming and not too many people.

When I got to the southernmost point, I ditched the bike in a roadside stand of rosehips and hiked my way through a quarter mile of poison ivy and prickers. I had thought the salt water would wash away all the ivy oil, but I was wrong. Two days later I was puffed up like a street junkie and scratching myself bloody in my sleep. But before then, I got to the bluff and scampered down it. Because of the difficult access, there was no one on the beach apart from a couple flabby nudists and a squat wolfman-looking dude with a walking stick. I swam in the surf, lay in the sun, drew things in the sand. After about an hour or so, I started thinking about ferries home. And that's when she showed up with her big purple towel and a backpack full of still-cold Bud.

She was tall and blond and twenty-two-ish, and she took off her striped suit and offered me a beer. We drank and talked, and the whole time she stood right next to me. Her tits looked heavy, and she brushed me with them when she turned to point out the lighthouse. Twice. Both into and out of the point. They were surprisingly cool. She said she was a waitress and it was her day off. She lay down on her towel and offered me a spot beside her. She had the kind of little gold watch you had to squint at to read and a tattoo of a moon sliver on her hip that she covered up with a stone. I lay down beside her, pretending she was mine until that wasn't enough. It's never enough. "Cut it out, okay?" she said. "What are you trying to do to me?" I asked her. "What are *you* doing to *me*," she corrected. But I still couldn't keep my hands off her. "Oh, all right," she said at some point—I had lost track of time—"it's my day off." So I climbed on top of her, and it was over pretty quick. After that we went for a swim and shared the last of her beers and watched the sun go down, and I finally started to feel the tight heat of my sunburn, but not all the ivy I'd cut through to get there. I wanted another shot, but she snorted and said, "You're just a kid. And it's my day off." So I put my head in her lap and looked up at the bottoms of her golden tits, and she scratched the sand out of my hair and looked out at the sea and drank the last of her now-warm beer.

Of course none of my friends believed me when I told them about it at the beginning of the school year. I should've never mentioned that she was a rich girl. That was one turn of the key too many. But she was. You could tell by the watch, and most of all by the notion that nothing bad would come from getting completely naked next to a strange teenage boy with bad teeth who swam in cutoffs and a belt. "Why didn't you stab her?" was all my buddy Justin McGuff had said. "I did," I said. "With my dick." Last I heard, McGuff had backslid pretty hard and was living underneath the old Fall River exit off 95. Camp Runamuck, they call it. I hope they never tear it down. He once sent me a postcard from a New Hampshire sober house:

Hey Nolan

Still fucking made up rich cunts on the beach you jerk?
Ate a chicken omlet for lunch and feel like shit.
No drugs. No nothing. More things should come in cans.
And not just chicken you fucking chicken.

You're pal McGuff

Thinking back, I'm not sure how he got it to me, the card, because while he very well might've been sober at the time, I sure wasn't. Must have sent it care of my mom. She used to leave things for me in the milk box—breakfast bars, smokes, mail, I guess, although I've never gotten all that much mail—because in those days Pop said he would shoot me if I ever came around, and he would've. But unless he heard loud cars, Pop never really got out of his chair, let alone stuck his head through the blinds to see who was on the porch.

4/19/01

My mom used to let me manhandle her a little. When Pop was at the doctor or maybe a bar, we would share the sofa and watch something on the tube—maybe an old movie or a talk show. The game. A cartoon, even. It didn't matter. My mom was usually so zonked that she would sort of fall asleep no matter what it was or what time it was. And she would snap off her work bra and pull me closer and I would touch her breasts, feel the weight of them through her shirt. Once or twice I got in bed with her and hassled her there. Until one day they were gone. I assumed that it was my fault. Now I know a little better.

4/23/01

Since you're likely curious, and since this will likely be my last entry, a few words on prison. It's probably all you ever wanted to hear about. You want it all to be so simple and so dirty, so you can say, "See?" Believe me, I know all about people like you and what you want.

But anyway, prison.

After three more or less sleepless weeks in Medium, I got sent down to Minimum, where I could breathe a little and where I met Teach, who was once a real teacher—in case you hadn't figured that out—then a bookstore clerk, then a yard worker, and, when I met him, a prison librarian. And after that, an ex-con. You could tell he had lost some of his smarts—it was like he was always looking for his keys inside his head—and it only got worse. But even so, Teach got me to read all kinds of things that got me thinking—the god-is-dead guy, the visible-invisible-man guy, the man-on-the-train guy. I owe him a lot. Thanks, Teach. The books helped.

5/11/01

Ed St. Germain is one of two barber-pole barbers left on the East Side, the other being his brother Fred. They both keep their shops on the same Wayland Avenue block even though they haven't talked since they put a man on the moon. I go to Ed's because he takes his time and can either bust balls or not bust balls. Fred's I've never liked: bright lighting and three or four guidance counselors waiting their turn, reading the sports section or police report. Fred's is strictly for bald guys.

I usually just get the boy's summer regular—a no. 7 clipper job with straight razor and warm foam finish—every couple months all year long. But today I wanted something special.

"The usual," Ed said after I climbed into the chair and he fitted me with the apron.

"Actually, this time I think I'd like something different."

"Oh yeah," he said, clipping the collar over the tissue paper.

"I was thinking maybe a real short cut, but with scissors and no clippers."

"Short? Short how?"

"You know, short all around, all the same length." I pulled my hand from under the apron and drew a halo around my head.

"Like with clippers," Ed said, wrinkling his nose at a scissor blade and selecting a different set of shears from a jar of Barbicide.

"Yeah, but no clippers. Longer than that, but still short. You know, like Steve McQueen."

"Steve McQueen."

"Yeah. Short like that."

"I can do that, but then you're not gonna like it. So I'll have to do it all over again with the clippers. Then who's the asshole?"

"No. I'm gonna like it."

"No you're not."

"Sure I will."

"Look. If I use scissors, it's gonna take too long and you're gonna look like goddamn Plum Mary. And then I'm gonna have to do it all over. You'll get a clipper cut like always."

"Yeah, but I don't—"

"Give it time. It'll grow out just like Spartacus, I promise."

"Steve McQueen," I mumbled, looking straight ahead.

"Same difference," Ed said, and pumped the chair to hair-cutting height. I leaned back and let him start in on the same cut he's always given me and always will give me if he ever gets another chance: a boy's summer regular. The clippers whined, and I rested my shoulders against the worn vinyl chair.

5/12/02

Got back from Providence at dawn. Showered off the smoke and the haircut hairs. Still feel itchy, hollow, raw. Will replace rags and kerosene tomorrow.

Have to figure this will be my last chance to get some measure of peace, to be truly alone. Till then I'll just sit here on this rock in the middle of the water and think of people who aren't here and watch the falling sun bruise the sky like a fist. Maybe once or twice I'll catch it rising.

5/13/02

Put away bedding.
Cleared downspouts.
Primed soffits.
Will stain tomorrow if weather holds.

(......)

CARETAKER: BACK WHEN THE MAYS FAMILY WAS CLOSER AND wealthier, they spent their white pants months at Twinrock, drinking bay-cooled gimlets and puttering away at any number of "projects." (The Mayses are tool-using WASPs from way back.) But given the high cost of upkeep and gin's tendency to loosen tongues and boil blood, since the mid-'70s the family has instead rented out their birthright to richer families. It's listed in *Yankee* magazine's most recent real estate section at eight grand a week. Nevertheless, every Memorial Day weekend the Mays family still throw their so-called Whitewash Party, whereat all the youngest family members and their school chums* are invited to spend three days and two nights out on the 'Rock, fixing shutters and drinks, staining the deck and the sheets, painting and getting some trim. All for the cost of thirty cases of Rolling Rock, six handles of Gordon's and twelve of Mount Gay. To augment this yearly upkeep, they also, until very recently, employed—to the tune of a hundred bucks a week plus whatever passes for room and board on a water-locked, weather-beaten, and by some accounts haunted rock—a winter caretaker. Now they rely on volunteers and uninvited guests like myself. Seems Rob was the last straw. Providing marginal types with second chances was one thing, harboring known fugitives quite another.

*And teachers. Eli attended only one Whitewasher. It was the spring of '89, and some guy whose face was shades redder than his faded red cap put his loafer up on a bolt of mothy sailcloth and raised his glass to the greenish setting sun. "Friends!" he said, beaming, "the first sunset of the season! Look!" Eli looked instead at all the people clapping and, his heart in his skull, climbed onto the roof. "It's not yours!" he shouted into the night, over all the cheers and ice and jokes. He steadied himself with the weather vane. "You can't own everything!" He paced and paced and at some point before dawn rowed ashore.

Carpenter Street: Carpenter is a crooked nine-block street just off Broadway on the West Side. The "goon's club" and a small bakery with no sign and strange hours—5:00 a.m. till whenever the pizza strips sell out—are all that's left of Carpenter Street's Italian roots. At the west end there's some kind of home—AIDS and drugs or just plain nuts; at the east a string of battery and muffler shops; and in between a neighborhood bar friendly to dogs and pairs of dog moms alike—with X on the juke, Sox on the tube, microbrews on tap, and 'Gansett* in cans: the kind of place where at one table you can talk redistricting with freelance photographers or adjuncts and at the next score Mob coke cut with Similac.

Short for Narragansett Lager, New England's premier cookout beer ("Hi, Neighbor! Have a 'Gansett," went the jingle) until Falstaff bought them out and started brewing it with Rust Belt tap. Beer-cap rebuses were the one good thing to come from this brief merger. I mean, who doesn't enjoy a good puzzle?

*Eli thought beer was for putting out fires, but his students liked it, so he always kept some on hand. When we cleaned out his last place, the fridge contained half a Halloween-themed six-pack of something they had stopped making a long time ago. SAVE FOR JAKE OR WHOMEVER read an index card taped to the carton. This would've hit me even harder if it weren't for the circle of at least a year's worth of butts and ashes an arm's length from his creaky nun's chair. I swept them into a pile the size of the cat I now wished I'd bought him. A Siamese, maybe. Or a Manx. She would have torn around the place first thing and knocked mugs off counters. She would have been curious, demanding, wary as hell.

Fox Point: The "wrong," or eastern, end of Providence's Fox Point is a neighborhood that, despite bordering both old and middle-aged money, has stayed just run-down enough for all kinds of down-on-their-luckers to call it home: single moms, day-job-holding night-school students paying their own way, too-old-for-rock-but-too-drunk-for-work rockers, Eli. And despite all odds, you'll still find more than a few Madonnas in bathtubs and a handful of old-for-Portuguese men* drinking the green wine they make themselves out of the thick-skinned Concords that hang from their carport grape arbors. The tenements are mostly vinyl-sided and have windowless hollow-core front doors with knob locks. A few blocks in any direction but due east into the Seekonk River, and things get swank quick.

*Fifty. Sixty tops. All that chourice does a number on a man's heart and guts. I went to grade school with a from-India

Indian kid who called them Pork-and-Cheese, which is mean but accurate.

Brown Plant Ops: Eager to spend the summer of my junior year outside of my increasingly crotchety grandfather's employ (*see subsequent note re: "Ike Hafkin['s] . . . kid"*), I, too, scored a job at Plant Ops. I took service calls, filled out repair requests, and radioed them to the appropriate on-duty tradespeople. Determining the exact nature of even the most mundane service problem was harder than it looked. On two separate occasions, and at opposite ends of the campus, two accentless undergrads referred to their torn window screens as "nets." You can imagine the knots they tied themselves into trying to describe things like jambs and muntins. In between calls I passed the time by browsing a decade's worth of logged service requests and redacting those I myself had made. In response to my next-to-last report of an oft-clogged suite toilet, one Manny Gomes had written the following note:

STUDENT PRODUCES EXCEPTIONALLY HARD TURDS.
PROBLEM WILL FIX ITSELF UPON GRADUATION.

All this sitting and looking back didn't exactly help matters. So instead of calling in Critter Control on an otherwise sleepy Monday holiday afternoon—VJ Day*—I forwarded the phones to the heat plant and strode over to Woolley Hall to see about a "huge, spitting spider" a couple girls had called in, screaming. When the sixteen-year-old summer sessioners found me, grinning, gripping a tow sack and a can of Black Flag, they screamed even louder, slammed the door, and dialed Campus Security, who squealed up and escorted me to the Brown jail cell I hadn't even known existed. I spat on the floor and demanded to speak to my dead parents' lawyer till they finally let me go, suddenly unsure of their right to hold a student against his will for knocking on a dorm room door.

The following day, I reminded my superiors that they would've had to pay Critter Control *double* time and half, given the holiday—and that the two girls might well have been poisoned by the time they had actually shown up. They told me that noting, let alone acting upon, such contingencies was most decidedly *not* in my job description. I told them that I was trying my best, and they mentioned that they had security footage of me taking things from the break room fridge and also of secreting the Freshman Crush Book into the men's growler at least twice a shift. I asked them if I could clear out my locker after supper, as I had ordered a large Hawaiian and a side of crazy bread, and they said I should just box that up, too.

> *Victory over Japan Day. An odious former national holiday ahistorically commemorating Japan's surrender in World War II. Currently celebrated only in Rhode Island—hell, even *Arizona* dumped it at some point—and not because we're a bunch of jingoistic yahoos, but because we would never abide the loss of a three-day weekend in August.

Hank LaChance: A schoolboy hockey legend in the early '60s, the former Central Falls High center and team captain, in the final sixteen seconds of by far the biggest game of his young career (the state finals against archrival Mount St. Charles), accidentally shot and scored on his own net, breaking a zed-zed tie. He promptly dropped out, put on weight, and began demolishing turkey coops in nearby Cumberland. After a full decade of drifting, a twenty-nine-year-old LaChance returned to CFH and all but begged his former coach, Clive Nolan, to hire him as an assistant, which he did as he did everything: begrudgingly. A mere two months into his homecoming, Hank began "dating" Clive's seventeen-year-old daughter, Louise—a senior—in the equipment room mostly, but also under the bleachers and at least once in the backseat of his late-model Maverick, which starry-eyed Louise mistook for the GT Fastback Steve McQueen drove in *Bullitt*. Hank is *deuxième génération poubelle blanche* from Woonsocket, which means part Maliseet Indian, so his folks spoke mainly English but with French phrasing, as in *throw me down the stairs, my hat*; *drive slow your car, you*; and *what is it now, this shit?*

. . . *forgot to hose down the side we had just heat-stripped*: I can only imagine what their premiums must be. In the past fifteen years, there have been three break-ins; the two car crashes, of course;* and, as Rob explains here, a fire. One would think it is cursed. And it very well may be. This is, after all, the same house in which Edgar Allen Poe failed not to drink, thus ending his engagement to a local poetess he had met while recovering from a recent suicide attempt. That view of a brick wall couldn't have helped poor Poe any.

After the first such crash, on November 14, 1992, Eli was sentenced to twenty-seven months at the Cranston-based Adult Correctional Institution for aggravated vehicular assault. According to court transcripts, just prior to the attack Eli brewed himself a pot of stronger-than-recommended-on-the-side-of-the-can coffee and poured it into a vase along with seven crushed nutmegs, six tablespoons of blackstrap, some milk, a couple glugs of rum, and a little sherry "to jazz it up." A pint or so of the admixture sloshing in his guts, he climbed into the company pickup and sped over to, then down, College Hill. At the last second, Eli hit the brakes, jerked the wheel, and so wound up not in the targeted parlor, but in the mudroom of her next-door neighbor. When asked by the sentencing judge why he—an educated man with no criminal record, and one formerly entrusted with the minds and bodies of children, no less—would pull a stunt like that, Eli replied that Maile Weinsberg, whose house he *had* meant to crash into, hadn't let him use the john when, earlier that same day, he'd been hard at work in her backyard. "We can't have these people using our toilet," Ms. Weinsberg supposedly shouted downstairs to her husband and door-getter. "This is *not* a truck stop!"

*Former Fox parent Phyllis Deinhardt. Mother of future Eagle Square project manager (*see note below, viz. ". . . mill building"*) Jacob Deinhardt, an ex-student against whom Eli held not even the slightest grudge, and whom, in fact, he kind of liked in spite of Jake's having also had a thing for teacher's erstwhile heavy pet, Alix. In the end, it was Mrs. Deinhardt's cherished fieldstone hearth that kept Eli from plowing straight through that wrong house, down the hill, over one of our smallest and least photogenic national parks, and into the Moshassuck River.

Ike Hafkin . . . his kid [*sic*]: Yours truly. "What? So you're a bum too, now?" said Grandpa Ike, getting his lawyer on the horn.

. . . the idea to live in a mill building: On August 1, 1993, eight RISD undergrads and one local high school dropout (the same Cliff Hinson Rob refers to here) decided, after only a week or two of seemingly idle talk, to rent for a mere $950 a month the entire third floor of One Eagle Square,* a pre–Civil War textile factory located in the formerly industrial Olneyville section of Providence. Others—including Rob and Viv—soon joined them, renting subdivided spaces on the two floors above.

*The building had been zoned commercial/light-industrial—past tenants included sweatshops, records management firms, fire- and water-damaged office retailers, and, in the case of the first two floors of One Eagle Square, an indoor flea market—but in the beginning no one paid its new inhabitants any mind, mostly because of Olneyville itself: a Superfund site tucked into what was then an all-but-forgotten river valley on the west side of Providence. Back then, Olneyville was one square mile of mostly empty mills, underused off-ramps and railroad tracks, cold-storage facilities, lumberyards, pawnshops, and crammed tenements. Up until the real estate boom of the late '90s, what few on-duty cops drove by Eagle Square paid more attention to that Dunkin' Donuts on the corner than to all the loud music and unkempt art punks hanging out in the flea market parking lot.

. . . a local nuthouse: Butler Hospital. Though I can't speak for Rob's glazier friend, my own stay at Butler was brief but refreshing, thanks in large part to the lush, rolling lawns; mature elms, pin oaks, and tulip trees; and soothing views of both the Seekonk River and Swan Point Cemetery. One morning I fed a lost fawn saved-up Craisins® through the bars of my bedroom window. Her dirty little lips tickled my fingertips, and I laughed like a child. After this book is done, I may well check myself back in. So many old faces. It would be reunion of sorts.

. . . a girl named Viv who wasn't a junkie yet: Alix's former Fox classmate Vivian Goddard (*see also "Exes," "Class History," "Neoteny"*).

Teach: Rob was my brother's last—and maybe best—student. I'm sure they made the most of the prison library's meager offerings. So little fiction . . .

Juárez: Whether this happened or is just something Eli made up or stole from a dynamiter's memoir almost doesn't matter. Or, should I say, doesn't mean it isn't revealing. Over the years, my brother had to tell a lot of stories and make up a lot of characters—heroes and villains alike—just to get by. And although I can't see him in

Mexico, that likely has more to do with the failure of my imagination than the wildness of his. And hell, either way, he probably believed it.

She was tall and blond . . . : You know, this sounds an awful lot like my sis, right down to the big nude boobs and the backpack of swill and the corny moon tattoo . . . I will stick to my earlier promise to leave her out of this, but I imagine many kid brothers go to some lengths to steal glimpses of their naked big sisters. And what's a little poison ivy? The sun and surf took its toll, of course—these coastal outdoors can be cruel to exteriors—but back in the day, she was something else. Even the negative spaces she made when silhouetted by the sun were hot.

Exes

Alix Mays

I GOT HOME FROM WORK—BREAKFAST SHIFT, BACK-TO-BACK Expository classes—to find a former student spread-eagled on the kitchen table.

"Hi dear," my mom mumbled through her paintbrush. She took it out of her jaw and stuck it into a blob of pink. "Come on in," she said, like there were way more than one of me and some of us weren't paying attention.

Fuck, I thought, plopping my things on the foldout Rob had liked to fuck on. It had been three weeks since I gave him the boot and two since my mom showed up, announcing that she needed a place to live and that she was painting vaginas. "I'm painting vaginas now," she said. "Fine," I said. But presently I must've sighed, because my mom—who I call Kit—shot me a look through her glasses, which, because they're thick and dark, is a look you only feel. I felt it.

"Hey Professor Mays!" my ex-student said, smiling. Kim? Too close to Kit, but stories where names can't get crossed are like sitcoms where no one says goodbye before they hang up. Kim wore a T-shirt, and her vulva was pointed at us. I could see why she might want to show it off. Instead, I looked at the canvas, where Kit had painted a hoofprint on a birthday cake. At least she put towels down.

"Alix, honey," I said, pushing Kit's wine-stained teacup away from the edge of the coffee table with my foot. "It's always been Alix."

"Alix." She laughed. "Your mom's an amazing artist!"

Kit frowned, knifed on some mauve, and tried to look at Kim over her glasses.

"Kit is . . ." I said, and went into my bedroom to grade essays. I sat on the bed, next to the Rob-shaped dent, and put the stack on my lap, but I couldn't grip a pen without fire up to my elbow. I threw the stack onto the floor, asked myself how old I was. Out on the fire escape I rubbed my bad hand with my okay one.

I still tell myself Rob had only been crashing, this latest time. That he just needed a place to call home because of the eviction. We'd broken up then, too. But this time was for good, and I meant it. He wore me out. I didn't even want to think about him anymore. "That's enough now," I told him, like I would in French—*ça suffit maintenant*—but in English. For real. *Ça . . . suf . . . fit.*

Outside, there wasn't much new to look at, apart from a silk-screened poster wheatpasted to a utility pole. It was of an empty, hivelike dress being picked at or else mended by crows. Even from where I sat, I could tell it was the work of an ex-friend—we were meant to. She was also Rob's ex, but that's not why we were ex-friends. We were ex-friends because of yet another ex—my first, who she didn't approve of. You can't ever get to the bottom of something by talking about one breakup. Providence is small; avoiding one another isn't easy.

You could see all the way down to three paint jobs ago on the triple-decker across the street: ochre, mint green, the red we call brick but that looks like dried blood. The clouds, meanwhile, were low and ragged, like old milk dumped into car-shop coffee. I watched them come together and break apart.

Then the Kim or whoever just about skipped to her car—the color of the sky, almost, but metallic—and I climbed back inside and waited for Kit to clean up. I closed my eyes and sang a five-minute song in my head, with pauses for where only guitars would be. I tried to sway to them, like I would if I were all alone.

In the kitchen, Kit was sticking her brushes into a yolk-crusted egg cup perched atop the day's tower of mugs and burnt pots of grain and bowls of watery cereal milk. When it fell over, she picked up the unbroken wineglass, wedged it against the side of the sink, held it upright with an ice pack, and shoved in her brushes. When she was done, I tried to rinse out the cereal bowls, but couldn't hold on to them.

"Kit," I said, rubbing my elbow. Did I want her to notice? Maybe. But it helped, and it's not like I made a big show of it.

"Yes, dear," she said, looking at something else.

"Could you do me favor and not leave your brushes in the sink."

"I need this, right now."

"I know you do, but—"

"I don't know that you do know."

"With you losing the house."

"There's nothing left!" She took her glasses off her head and used them to cover her eyes. "So many still have it in for us," she said.

"Rob—"

She made one of her faces.

"Yeah, well—sure," I said. "But we split the rent."

"I need to focus on my work right now." Kit stroked the arm of the couch like it was a cat's back, then picked at it like that cat's mother.

"I know Twinrock's cold—" I said.

"Fud hired someone."

"There's money for that?"

"Oh, he'll never pay."

"Right. But that's not . . ." This is where we always wound up, with long-standing feuds and torts and grievances, with exquisite corpses constructed from diary entries and hostile notes left on counters or tacked to bedroom doors. I took a breath. "I'm talking about brushes in the sink. I'm talking about staring directly into my former student's vulva, first thing when I get home from teaching, and I also worked breakfast."

Kit opened her mouth, but I put up my hand.

"Oh, and I almost said *cunt*, okay? That's how pissed I am. I don't want to think of vulvas as cunts. I don't want to think of my students' genitals, period."

"And last spring," she said, like she was in the middle of a speech I had walked in on, "I stood naked in a room full of strangers in the desert and talked about my life." She smoothed the couch-fabric pills she'd plucked up. "For the first time, I felt like myself. Like how I felt before all this. Before my shitass father lost control. And Fud, too. Before all these men. Your father . . . Before the fall."

I could smell the wine she snuck. I swore I could still smell Kim too, though I hadn't before. I closed my eyes and saw that illustration of Alice in Wonderland's neck stretching—of her growing too big for the room. The drawing used to keep me awake as a kid, so with a flourish, Kit would remove the book from my shelf before shutting the light. Like it *was*, in fact, the book's fault. I called her Kit back then, too. "I may be your mother," she would say, "but I am *not* a *mom*." It was joke. But she meant it.

"Look, Kit, I know how hard it is and how hard it must've been, but I have some needs here, too."

"And what makes you think these needs are somehow graver than mine? Whatsoever gives you that idea?"

"This is my house!"

"I have no home!"

"Fuck! I know!"

"Do you know my baby brother's going to prison?"

"Yes."

"I want to celebrate something. Can you blame me?"

"That's not—"

"So you know her . . . this . . . *girl*. So what? She's not ashamed. You think you know so much."

"You don't even know her name."

Kit made the noise she makes when she knows I'm right. A wet little *k*, or a *ch* that sounds like *k*. Like *Chk*. "Look at your shame," Kit said. "You owe it to yourself. You owe it to me!"

When I realized she wasn't going anywhere—because she couldn't: she had nowhere to go—I grabbed my keys and left. It was still light out, somehow.

The poster announced the first in a series of so-called Monthly Spectacles, meant to celebrate the grand opening of Polyesther, a women's art collective that same ex-friend, Viv Goddard, had started in what had once been a knitted-underwear factory above a shuttered wig shop. Turned out those weren't birds on the poster, but cats dressed as rabbits. The dress was made entirely of tampons, of course. I smiled, or tried to, at least. I really wanted to smile. Oh, Viv, I thought. We used to make each other pee our pants. Looking over my shoulder at the impossibly tiny house where Kit was almost certainly not cleaning up, I found myself wishing I'd handled things differently over the years, that I hadn't burned quite so many bridges.

I heard the squeak of an outdoor faucet and the rush of water onto the street. I looked to my left.

"Hi, neighbor."

Georgie. I hadn't seen him in a couple days, and one can always hope, but no such luck. I turned to the right and walked, not too quickly but purposefully, toward something I'd figure out when I got there.

"Look, I'm your friend, okay?" Georgie said, shutting off his hose.

I kept walking.

"I'm your fucking friend!"

Faster.

"Alix!"

My name in his gross mouth stopped me, but I didn't turn around. "How do you know my name?" I said as calmly and firmly as I could.

"Your mother," he said.

I wanted to slap the glasses off her face, shake her. "Well, it's not yours to use."

"I'm just trying to be nice is all," he said. "This is both of ours neighborhood."

He wasn't wrong.

"Motherfucker," he said either at me or the hose, which came on all of a sudden. I walked as fast as I could without it becoming running.

For a split second—like when you come down hard on an expected but nonexistent stair—I caught myself missing Rob, but just as quickly remembered that I was more scared of how he would react to stuff like this than to the stuff itself. "You are choosing to live here," he said. "These are all choices you get to make," he added, hitting both the *you* and the *get*. I just wanted to know which was the first such choice. I just wanted to know where I went wrong.

I mean, I know where—meaning with whom—but I couldn't tell Rob. Not about Eli. Are you kidding? Rob would literally kill him.

But first I needed to find Kit someplace where she could spread out. Problem was, my apartment was too little and Kit only had new friends. Once, when I asked her whatever became of the latest someone I liked but all of a sudden never saw anymore, she said, "Oh, she got old." This someone was thirty, but I was sixteen, so I didn't know how to respond yet. I must've made a face, because Kit sniffed. "Well, I happen to like young people. They're not . . .

stuck." She pushed those exact same glasses up her nose, her mouth a small, tight O. Stuck. Stuck. *Stuck.* It sounded like onomatopoeia. In another few years I'd know firsthand that it was. Now, at the corner, I said it aloud, "Stuck." There was another Polyesther poster. Jesus. They were everywhere. Around the corner, someone honked in front of someone else's house instead of getting out and ringing the bell.

Wait, I thought, why not? Kit's a lady. And an artist, I guess. And Viv will like her—like how she used to like me, maybe. I turned sharply west and walked down Broadway toward Olneyville Square.

Viv was a friend, my best friend, whatever that means or meant, but hadn't been since I started dating—by which I mean fucking—my first boyfriend, Eli, who was also my high school English teacher. "You have boys in your head," Viv told me more than once.

But first, three quick things about Eli before you get all bent out of shape. I don't care if you believe them:

1. It was love, not just lust. For Eli at least. For me it was lust, pretty much. He had puffy upper arms—which you either get or don't get—and smelled like Coke ingredients and just-opened-up lake house. Like the start of someone else's summer. Fuck you, that's how I felt. He also had eyes that looked like they were looking at something far away, except when they looked right at you, when they took you in. He loved me, and we both had a hard time saying goodbye. And in the end, that's what this is really about.
2. I'd turned eighteen the second week of the school year, before he probably even had my name down, so I was an adult. And he was just twenty-two.
3. Eli had my yes every step of the way, so, his contract and basic professional ethics aside, it wasn't wrong

> exactly, just weird, but even then only in retrospect. The first time around, you can't help but miss the point, and what isn't weird? Have you ever been to France? Or so much as talked with a French person about sex? *But how else are you supposed to learn*, they say. Plus, the word *weird* is boring and sad and says much more about the person who uses it than it does about the person, place, or thing it fails to describe. *Weird* and *closure* are the only nonracist or sexist words I won't let my students use. But I wouldn't let them get away with any of this. *Too much exposition*, I would write in the margins. Or else, *Discursive.* I'm all over the place. But then life is never chronological when you're trying your best to share it with someone else. Do as I say, I'd say, not as I . . . you know.

Twelve years ago, now. I didn't know who I was yet, but even so, it didn't take me long to realize that Eli didn't know who he was either and took the not knowing much harder than I did. He took most things hard. When we fought, which with time was more and more, he would tear his clothes and hit himself in the head as if he were hitting someone else. Since then I've learned that's just how addicts are, like two different people giving each other a hard time at the same time—that is if you're the kind of person who likes to look at people as collections of symptoms that can and should be treated, which I'm not sure I am.

But this was about Viv.

When I met her, she carried her things in a construction worker's lunch box, even her art, increasingly the only thing of hers not covered in paint splatters. The big black boots she showed up with at the beginning of sophomore year were splattered white within a week, but her drawings and photos were small and clean and curled into tubes. We had no classes together, but I smiled at her in the hallway once or twice. She smiled back. There was a telephone pole down the block from school. When we walked past it on our way to Thayer Street, we'd talk. We were friends past the pole. I told her about the pole. "I'm leaving in a week, you know," she said. She was transferring to a girls' school. There was the tampon incident, of course, but really she'd just had enough. Who could blame her?

"I know," I said, looking at my sneakers.

When she asked me why it took so long for me to talk to her, I said, "I didn't think someone like you would like someone like me."

"We can like who we want, you know. Wherever," she said, walking back to that pole to gouge an *X* into it with her keys. "Whenever."

The wig shop was still boarded up, so the front door to Polyesther was the back door to what hadn't been SyBell Underwear since the early '40s. What it had been between then and now was anyone's guess. A typing school? Methadone clinic? Boudoir studio? The door was propped open with a paint bucket. There was a black Sharpied note taped to it, decorated with stars and webs and butts. COME IN, it read.

The foyer was wallpapered with the repeated image of what turned out to be not an octopus devouring conjoined twins, but young lovers kissing beneath a wisteria-tangled gazebo. I said hello a couple times. From upstairs came sawing and something being dragged from one end of the room to the other, then back again. The banister was worn and burnished by years and years of hands, except for where splintery two-by chunks filled in gaps.

Upstairs was broken up into many tiny lofts. The windows that weren't boarded up were hung with curtains that used to be either black or red and looked like they'd been used in a school play to suggest a throne room or bordello. I followed the noises to what turned out to be the kitchen, identifiable only by the drawing on the wall of the stove they didn't have. Glued above it was an already grease-spattered mosaic of subscription recipe cards. A girl in flip-flops power-chiseled linoleum. Another, in boots, sawed through a piece of drywall. I didn't recognize either of them; they were young, cool. RISD? The women wiped sweat and nodded at me. I nodded back.

I was going to ask if they'd seen Viv, when I saw her by an un-boarded-up window in the far corner of what the tape indicated would soon be another room. I walked over, dragging my feet so as not to startle her. She looked up from the print she was screening of an old white guy suckling at the marble dome of the State Capitol. Crab claws and eyestalks poked from his breast pocket. "Sanderson & Sons" was written across his bald spot in curlicues that all but dared you to call them girly, and below him, in block print:

SAVE OLNEYVILLE!
FIGHT GENTRIFICATION!

"All right," Viv said, brushing dust off her Lizzy Borden T-shirt. She hugged me and then did that thing uncles do, where they hold the just-hugged person in place and lean back to look at them. But her eyes were overpoured drinks.

"Viv," I said, and gave her a smile.

"I'm glad! Why are you here?"

"Well . . . you know . . ." I suddenly realized this was a question I hadn't rehearsed an answer to on the walk over. "I just—I wanted to see how it was going?"

She gestured all around herself to show exactly how it was going. "Slowly, dirtily," she said.

"It looks great."

"It looks like someone locked Eagle Square in the attic." She smiled, either at the place or her simile.

She asked what I was up to these days, and I told her about my jobs. She told me about her new work, about how it was theatrical, about how it lived in the moment. "We have enough stuff to last us lifetimes," she said. "Do you still have those pictures we took? In the old house? Of you and me?"

"No."

"Whatever happened to them?" The difficult-thought wrinkle at the bridge of her nose didn't fade right away.

I couldn't tell her. "Oh, you know. Moving . . . Moves."

"All that back and forth?" The wrinkle was gone now. "They'll have to carry me out of here on a stretcher."

"You don't have the negatives?"

She gestured around the place again, as if to say, who could find them if she did.

I told her about Kit, and how she was painting now, and how she needed somewhere to live, leaving out the Vagina Project and everything else.

"There's no plumbing upstairs, but we still have a couple spots left. I have to say that I like the idea of layered generations. Can she do taxes?"

"No."

"Can she bake bread?"

"She's good to talk to, sometimes."

"Some of us need help with that."

I gave her Kit's business card, which I was surprised I even had, let alone on my person and in the first place I looked. Kit couldn't afford anything but the plain white kind, so had soaked them all in Lady Grey. I crossed out her old number, replaced it with my new one, and handed the card to Viv. She turned it over in her hands.

"You and Jacob Deinhardt are friends, right?" asked Viv.

She meant Jake, who only kind of took her place after she had transferred and before Eli. I hadn't thought of him in years.

It made me feel bad all of a sudden. "Now? No, not really . . . Not anymore."

"I mean, you were—right? In high school."

"Yeah, well—I guess. I needed someone to hang out with." Once I realized I was rubbing my hand—because it hurt—I stopped.

"Well, he works for Sanderson and Sons." She gestured at her poster. "He's their lead on the Eagle Square project."

"We haven't spoken in years," I said, truthfully. "Not since college."

"College," Viv said, looking at her now-dry print as if she still had choices to make. I looked at her looking at it for as long as felt normal. I started to make well-I-better-get-going noises. "I'll be in touch," she said. "With your mom."

"Great," I said. But it was great. I mean, it was something. It felt good?

Once Viv had left Fox for the Jane S. Dorr School for Young Ladies, she would cut class and meet me on my frees to smoke pot and shoot the shit and take pictures. Viv was just getting into photography. And that's when we found our favorite hangout: a steep, block-long street lined with abandoned tenements that dead-ended near the foot of the Prospect Park wall. We didn't know the story behind the tenements, but it looked like they hadn't been lived in since the sixties. There were four: identical triple-deckers set close together on one side of the street, opposite a sloping vacant lot filled with wind-strewn trash and, in the summertime, broom corn and sumacs. The chain-link fence surrounding it was low and kicked-in, and you could tell from all the empty coolers and cracked whippets that kids partied there at night.

We walked up and down the street a bunch of times, peeking through cracked and boarded windows before we worked up the nerve to break into one of the houses. Viv brought her camera, like always, and I had swiped a crowbar from Buildings and Grounds, but it turned out we didn't need it, because the back door to the house at the very top of the hill was unlocked. There was only a hole where the knob had once been, and the door swung open easy. The stairwell was pitch-black. Viv led the way by feeling along the wall while I held on to her waist, which came and went beneath the thin fabric of her dress. I didn't know I could still get scared like that, like a little girl. The fallen chunks of gouged-out plaster made gritty noises beneath our feet.

The third-floor apartment was dark despite long shafts of dust-spangled daylight that spilled in through the many missing windows. The splintering floorboards were streaked with bat or pigeon shit and buckled beneath our feet as we walked. "This is perfect," Viv kept saying, clicking pictures. "Just perfect." Wallpaper hung off the walls in great crumbling sheets, like bark peeling from a birch's trunk.

Viv stepped back from the dust-coated mantel. "Here," she said, taking off her dress, "put this on. I'll get a shot of you in the fireplace, crouching, reaching up."

I took off my jeans and everything else. My skin felt hot and cold at the same time. Viv handed me her dress. I was about to slip it on when she said, "Wait. Lie down on the floor first, in front of the fireplace. For a second." I found a splinterless and only just dusty spot and did as she said, my eyes closed the whole time. One camera click, two clicks. "Okay. Get up now." Viv and I looked at the cleaner spot my left thigh and ass and shoulder had left behind. "Perfect," she said, and on a super-slow exposure clicked the picture that still hangs above my mantel. "Now put on the dress and reach up the chimney."

Once again I did as Viv said, crouching down on the balls of my feet, steadying myself with one arm, reaching up with other. I felt soot-caked brick with my outstretched fingertips. I swallowed the lump rising in my throat, clamped shut my eyes and mouth, and lifted up my head. The inside of the chimney was black, airless, and webbed with dust. Something brushed against my cheek and clung to my hair. I imagined the wings of clustered bats against my skin. I waited for one to wake up, to flap its wings. I held my breath for as long as I could.

Now I was late for class and had nothing to hand back. Eli told me he always used to keep a spare lesson in a drawer—so to speak; he had no desk, just his lap and wherever he sat—so he could always whip something out at the last minute. His stashed lesson was on kleptomaniacal breakfast cereal mascots—*Lucky! Trix! Sonny! Cookie Crook! And what exactly are these Cinnamon Crunch Toast Bakers doing in our kitchen so early in the morning? What are we so goddamned afraid of?* But I figured I'd teach my class about Proust's madeleine and about how their senses can take them back to their childhoods. Pretty half-assed, but it was just meant to be something to get them thinking, by which I mean talking and maybe writing, because Expository is just a class. But right away they got hung up.

"I can't picture the cookie—is it shaped like a girl?" My hand-raisingest student asked.

"You get them at Starbucks," another guy said. "They're like Twinkies without the cream filling. And look like a clam or something."

"Like a door knocker you mean," another kid added. "A fancy door knocker."

"Do Twinkies make any one else's fingers burn?"

Everybody laughed.

"Okay," I said. But it was too late. Everybody was talking about Twinkies now, and how they wouldn't rot. I looked around the room for a way out.

One woman, who sat in my blind spot—or immediate left, if you're not a teacher—raised her hand. I was so excited, I called on her before her arm was fully extended.

"In middle school, after school, I'd always come home and eat a salad with Catalina Dressing in front of *General Hospital*, and now just the sight of it makes me want to throw up."

"That's so crazy," shouted a girl from the back row who never talked. "In middle school I ate a salad *on* Catalina with an actor *from General Hospital*! And I could've thrown up!"

"We're like twins," went the first girl.

We all laughed, except for them. Because it wasn't funny. But I didn't realize why not until after class let out. Shit, I thought. If I'm not careful, I'll get caught up in the moment, too. That's the hardest part about being a teacher: always keeping one eye out.

Eli thought of me as a woman before anyone else did, though everyone thought he liked me because I wasn't one yet. When I was growing up, kids and adults—my family, really—called me a tomboy because I liked to climb and dig and was long and ropy like a boy. I much prefer the French expression *garçon manqué*, missed boy, or maybe failed boy, a phrase that better describes my exes than me. The French can feel the presence of an absence like no one else.

Right before Christmas break, Eli invited all of us over to his place to watch a film he had scolded us for not even hearing of, let alone seeing, likely knowing that only Jake and I would show up. "In France, even nine-year-olds drink wine," Eli said, pouring all three of us a glass of Bordeaux in his slant-ceilinged attic apartment. "Just like the Fonz!" Jake had said when we first walked in. "In a Very Special Episode," he now added, staring into the wine he wouldn't finish.

We followed Eli's lead and raised our glasses. "But no brushing till you're twelve!" he said. And we watched *Claire's Knee* or *Le Rayon Vert*, I can't remember which.

During free periods and on weekends we all started taking walks together and pretty soon smoking weed. By the time Eli began ditching Jake or else sending him on lost-cause scavenger hunts—*Say, can a guy still find wax lips round here?* Or, *We need Canned Heat to clean the hookah. Jake!*—I knew.

Eli was the first man to tell me I was beautiful. I was going to say the first man other than my father—who I called Ned—but that isn't true. Ned's preferred word was *gorgeous*, but he used it as a proper noun, as in, *Hey there, Gorgeous. How was your day?* After Eli said it, I didn't say anything. Jake was off looking for sorghum or a box of cocktail swords, and my cheeks were hot from wine and my tongue suddenly felt like leather in my mouth.

Maybe I could see it now—what Eli saw in me—in those photographs Viv took. But Eli has them. All I have is the one of my body shape on the floor. It hangs in my bedroom just above the sealed-up fireplace. Still, I waited till Rob was gone to take it out. He would've recognized me, and he was that jealous. I never even told him about Eli, because of how he grew up. He would've gotten it all backwards. The French use the same word for *backwards*, *inside out*, and *upside down*; they communicate with metaphors and syntax. With their bodies and their voices.

But even back then, I dragged the photos out only when people asked. People meaning Eli. This was before we had fucked. Like everyone else allowed in my room, he saw the photo on the wall and asked the same questions everyone asks, more or less. Jake was there. He'd already seen the pictures, but had since come to resent that I had shown them to him, I think—like I thought he was a eunuch or something for trusting him with my nude image. And it's true: I never once considered so much as his most general physical desires. But when Eli asked to see the other pictures, Jake said, in a small voice that I hated, "No. Don't do it, Alix." I wanted to punch him when his voice got small like that.

"Don't worry," Eli said. "I won't tell."

So I did, while Jacob worried his cuticles in the corner and, later, the hallway. Then, at some point, he just left. Kit likely didn't see him out, as she never quite knew who he was or what I saw in him.

"These . . . are . . . *beautiful*," Eli said, looking at the pictures. Now, in my mind's eye and ear, I can see and hear the fear in his eyes and voice as he lingered over those black-and-whites of Viv and me. We thought we were really onto something. Well, weren't we? She was. But now I'm writing about it, and she's onto something else, and they don't call it the last word for nothing. "Viv's got some eye," he said.

Later, Eli got up to pee—or take a leak or piss, he would've corrected: "Only girls and babies pee," he liked to say, "grown men relieve themselves transitively"—and I followed him into the hall bathroom, because in old houses that's all there is. So he took it out and I looked at it, and nothing happened. "It's hard with you watching. I mean, difficult."

I turned my back for a bit. Long enough for a stream to start, at which point I turned around. "When you're done, can I tap it off?" I asked. "I've heard about tapping off."

"Okay," he said. "That's fair. The exchange rate oughta be lousy."

When he finished, I tapped it off. Then I led him over to the sink and mixed the water in my other palm and rinsed him. He nodded at the soap, and I used it and let the water run, and afterward, while he dried himself off, I pulled the waste pull. It gurgled rudely.

Later, in my room, we kissed. Some things had to wait until I felt comfortable, which took longer than I had expected, but he stayed patient and kind. In the meantime, I just saw to his wants. Eagerly, like the star pupil it turned out I had always wanted to be, deep down.

Kit figured it out pretty much right away. But she didn't get mad. One afternoon, when Eli and I lay in bed, we heard a knock at the front door. Kit let Jake in, and he sat with her in the kitchen, which was just below my room. It sounded like he was there to see her. I listened through the radiator. His voice had gotten so low all of a sudden that I couldn't quite hear him. But Kit's voice was a bell. "Alix seems happy for a change. So let's keep this under our hats, Sam."

There was a pause, during which he corrected her, presumably. But politely.

"Up until now, I've never been able to describe my daughter as happy. Can you understand that, Jacob?"

Another muffled pause. I leaned in to where the pipe met the floor.

"It really is," she said, and looked at something I couldn't see. "Let's talk, Jacob. Sit. Can I fix you a drink?"

I heard heavy footsteps and then the front-door glass shudder.

And it didn't take long before other people started asking questions. *Ask,* I say, like they ever just *asked*. They only went, *Ew*, or *Ohmygod, are you okay?* Yeah, I said. I'm *fine*.

Ned and Kit had only been talking logistics since my idiot brother's expulsion. But for my folks things had soured long before that, back when Kit started dressing like a wizard—in loose tunics and robes with sleeves floppy enough to hide rabbits, baggy pants, little slippers, everything but the hat and beard. Women of a certain age will dress like wizards if their husbands haven't been paying close enough attention for long enough, regardless of how rich and pretty they were or are or still could be. "Mother warned me not to marry new money," Kit once told me over early-evening cups of vervain tea, just after my announcing that I had changed my last name to Mays—hers, meaning her father's, who was also an asshole, but what are you going to do? "Us Mayses are Jamestown through and through, and if anything, I should've married up. A Vanderbilt or a Haffenreffer. A Pell, even. Christ, Jordan Falleman was drunker than a shithouse rat, but at least he understood appearances. Leave it to a third-generation Mick like your father to out-country-club a WASP."

But it wasn't long before we moved on to my father's secretary, whom Kit and I were both convinced he was fucking because that's just what happens. She's more or less my age and we have pretty much the same silhouette, minus the tits. Kit smiled at me and said, "Well, they all have bigger tits. Some things oughtn't surprise you. Not at your age." I didn't hate my dad's secretary because of her looking like a more perfect me; you should never hate people for things they can't help. And she was just the latest in a series. Plus, ew.

So I can see now how Eli and his dirty poems and creepy music and perfectly puffy upper arms came along at just the right time for a girl like me with a dad like that. But unless you are a mathematician or a life coach, maybe, patterns are only so interesting. It's moments that I miss. A specific choice. A surprise.

Eli showed me all kinds of places cool to bored teenagers like me and overgrown teenagers like him—the then-unsealed train tunnel, the rusted-up drawbridge, the cursed fountain on Benefit, Lovecraft's grave: obvious spots, sure, but I was just a girl, and it was all still new to me, even though Viv had shown all of them to me first, a good six months before Eli had so much as brushed against my thigh.

A couple days later, after getting off a brunch shift, I stood outside my front door and listened to Kit and someone else inside, chatting but with the kind of gaps that indicate thought. I wasn't having a hard time with the key on purpose—it was fresh-cut; I had left my old one with Kit, not that she was going anywhere—but my struggles quieted them down all the same. I switched hands and managed, at last, to unlock the door, and it swung open on Kit and Viv, sitting on the couch, drinking what I should've known wasn't tea. Of course, the key was now stuck, so I had to stand there and jiggle it free while they sat and smiled at me from behind their cups.

"Hey, Alix," Viv said.

"Hi, dear," Kit said. "Why didn't you tell me what a hoot your friend was!"

Because she isn't my friend? I thought. And I did tell you? All through high school? Plus, you met? Twice? "That's great," I said, meaning it, because, again.

"We've been having such fun. And listen to this, there's a spot in her marvelous new collective. I could paint!"

"Oh, yeah?" I said.

"Her experience will go a long way," Viv said. "She'll be a big help."

They both smiled at me. Their teeth were black from wine. I could've cried.

Eli and I kept at it through the summer and into the next year, even after everyone found out about us, because Eli never stopped loving me, and at that point I was like, fuck you, to everyone else. I deferred enrollment at the Université Paris X-Nanterre for a year—even though it was too late to back out of the lease on the studio apartment in the Marais—and moved into Eli's new place, on Smith Hill. It was a grim one-bedroom on the third floor of what had once been a rich man's home. Presumably, this was where the help had lived. There was no door to our apartment, and a dog tied to a pole in the backyard—which was its bed and its toilet—and only one tree on the whole block, a honey locust that had been planted the year before, backed into from a couple different angles, and wouldn't make it through the winter. Eli took a job at the Borders in Cranston, and I became a nanny. We never got unpacked or put anything on the walls, and I never learned which way to turn the downstairs key, but to this day, if I smell something that smells even remotely like the shampoo we used then—which smelled like nectarines and their pits—or like the bread we bought, my throat cramps. "You will miss this," Eli had told me when we blew a fuse with our fan and the stereo and a lamp. "You will miss all of this," he said again, like a curse. Then we made our own noise in the dark, still air. *"Oui, oh, ouais,"* I said, practicing my French.

One morning in the late fall, after he had hit snooze for the third straight time—it was one of those weeks when he couldn't get out of bed, and he had them more and more—I sat up and squinted at his name tag on the kitchen counter, glary in the early morning sun, and I wanted to climb onto the roof and scream. So I did. The window slammed shut behind me, and I got shingle grit under my nails scooting up and behind a dormer. I screamed differently, and Eli got up and joined me, propping the window behind him with that year's doorstop hardcover. He didn't ask what I was doing, which made me realize why I loved him but also why I couldn't stay. "You know," he said, handing me the bowl he had packed at some point between getting up and climbing out the window, "I'm still not sure if I did or didn't fly to work all last week." His face was squinty and pale in the sun. I passed him back the bowl, and he took a hit. "Or if I did or didn't quit drinking." He looked at me, then exhaled. "I know I can't fly, but did I drink last week?"

He called in sick, which he was, and we spent the rest of the day smoking weed and making what felt like love. I was nineteen.

The next day, when he was back at work, I called Kit and told her I wanted to go to Paris after all, that Eli and I were through, and more or less why. "I just can't see myself with him," I said.

"Men live in the past," she said. "Women in the future."

"I thought men only cared about what they want right now."

"Oh, it's the past. They just act like it's the present, which is worse. Women, we can't help it. We're always looking ahead. Watch how we drive."

I packed my two suitcases till they could close only when I sat on them, but left most of what I owned behind, including that box of photographs, and I started to write a note but got lost in the words and my handwriting, which suddenly looked small and girlish and dumb, and shoved it into my pocket. So I left us—I mean Eli—a message on our machine, which was now *his* machine even though he'd never wanted it. "Do you think I'm afraid of missing things?" he'd asked me in the store. Buying the damned thing was my answer.

It took a couple tries. "It's me. Going out to the 'Rock," I said onto the tape, meaning Twinrock. "Will basically just leave for France from there. So, bye, I guess." On a piece of paper I wrote, "Eli—Listen to the message," and put it next to the phone along with the instruction booklet, which I had stashed in a drawer and luckily found. *Bye* had two syllables the way I said it over the phone—*by-eeeee*—and that was all I would admit to regretting for a long time, even though it immediately felt like I had vomited my heart. He was dead afraid to fly, so I figured that was it. I mean, that had to be it. This was exactly how and why I thought such things ended. My whole life was ahead of me. I was just a girl, right? I couldn't wait to get out. Nineteen.

On the plane, I cut all my food in half and just looked at it. I asked for a third and fifth wine and eventually got cut off. The last time we fucked, he had been late for work as usual, and I didn't come. On top of everything else, that must've killed him. "This isn't interesting," he'd say, holding up the fingertips of cum he'd just wiped from the wall or my belly. "I want to know about you." On the plane, while some lady slept beside me, I thought about the one time on the ski trip and on the bus ride back, and then the other time at school, behind the curtain during Quaker Meeting, and got myself off under my plastic-y airline blanket. I crackled with static. I turned on the air and pointed it at my head.

For the next three months I had what couldn't possibly still be jet lag. I'd fall asleep whenever and wake up early and suddenly. I lost track of time. It all felt like one long day. The heart I no longer had hurt.

The teacher in me is now writing *show don't tell* in the margins, but some things can't be seen. So you'll just have to take my word about how it felt. I felt broken. I wore thick-soled boots to make up for the height I felt I'd lost.

My place was a forty-five minute Metro ride from La Défense. School started up again in January, and I got lost in schoolwork and in people I had just met. It took my mind off. Okay, I thought, *this* is who I am. *This* is what I want. Look at these pictures I took in my head: Me at the Gare du Nord. Look. This is me at Beaubourg. And on the Rue des Rosiers, eating a merguez and trying not to make a mess. Tahini running up my arm. This is me avoiding *le 16ème*. This is me dancing however I dance at les Bains Douches. Two of Lenny Kravitz's flipped-back dreadlocks wind up in my mouth, and he yanks them out as if I had wanted them there. They taste like cigarettes and white musk. He sneers in my vicinity. Here I am in the Marais, at a party thrown by Claude Picasso or France Gall's son. Daughter? By Charlotte Gainsbourg? I can go home with anyone I want, I think. Meanwhile, I get good at telling guys on the street to go fuck themselves. "*Dégage, connard!*" I shout, loud and cold. I don't wear a short skirt in the nineteenth arrondissement. Never linger alone in public. I always look like I know where I'm going.

I heard different things about Eli. The bookstore fired him, he was gay, he was basically homeless. He exposed himself to a nurse. He spent a night in jail. I screen my calls, put his letters in a box, put the box in the closet. I laugh a lot in public. I laugh in French. I learn how to spit.

Tense slips, I'd now write. *Watch out.*

"Alix," Viv said once Kit had gone to the bathroom.

"Mmm-hmm," I said, pretending to be interested in something in the sink even though it was empty and clean, finally. I scrubbed it anyway.

"You're not going to want to hear this, but . . ."

I stopped scrubbing nothing. "Are you going to tell me?"

"It's about Rob."

"Oh, Christ—really, Viv? Rob?"

"Not about him—well, wait, no. I mean . . . It's about where he is."

"Jail? Detox?"

"Twinrock. He's the caretaker. Your uncle hired him."

My throat cramped.

"Kit didn't want to tell you," she said.

"But you did."

"Someone needed to. Do you really think I want to be talking about Rob?"

"I don't know what you want, to be honest."

"I'm trying to help."

"Got it." I picked up Kit's and Viv's cups and put them in the sink.

"It's okay," she said. "We both fell for him."

"Is that supposed to bring us together?"

She made a disgusted noise. "That's not what I mean. I mean—I just want to talk to you, okay? I want to see how you're doing."

"I'm going out," I yelled so Kit could hear me, ostensibly. Then I grabbed my old keys, and not my waist apron, and almost ran to the door.

"We all have our own messes, Alix," Viv said, her voice following me down the stairs. "We don't have to be friends past the pole!"

At the bottom of the stairwell I caught my breath and waited for the sound of Viv closing the door. I smelled like brunch.

In late March, in Paris, I got a call from the phone booth below my garret. "I'm outside," Eli said.

"Of what?" I asked.

"Look," he said. "I can see you. Across the street." I looked out the window. It was true. His grin was wild. He had hangover hair. He had flown? The least I could do was tell him the code to the front door, so I did. Then I looked in the mirror, lit a cigarette, and took out the copy of *I Would Have Saved Them If I Could* I bought at Shakespeare and Company, then put it back, then took it out again, then put it back. Then took it back out and left it there until Eli knocked, at which point I hid it under the latest *Marie Claire*. He found it later, and smiled. "Well, I'll be," he said, and sat down on my bed and poured himself another drink. He read me his favorite sentences, which were my favorite sentences, while I did something—anything—at the sink. I banged the teapot around while he read, wanting him to stop but also not to stop. My tea had tears in it. I didn't offer him any.

He stayed for three or six days that felt like a year and a half. We fought where people usually fucked, and fucked where people did neither. He fucked me in the sink, banging his head where the ceiling slanted with the roof. We barely left the apartment. When we did, he bought me a scarf that I would later make a point of using only to stop the door gap when smoking pot, or hash, actually. In Paris we all smoked hash. I was just trying to look tough for my new friends. There were new ones almost every week. I forget more names than I remember. The scarf smelled like horse and roses and gasoline and was covered with little mirrors that could cut you and got snagged on whatever else you or someone near you was wearing, but it made hundreds of little whoever-was-looking-right-at-you's and wildly caught the light from across the room or street and flashed it back at them like something they weren't meant to see but were thrilled they had. On the way back from the market Eli tore it off me and wrapped it around his neck and ran, laughing, an explosion of the whitest light in a rare sliver of afternoon sun. I laughed so hard people gave me dirty looks. I shot them right back, threw in "*Ta gueule.*"

On what turned out to be our last day in Paris, we fought about me telling him exactly how many men I had fucked since I left home—nine, eighteen, if you counted everything but—just because he hadn't asked. I had wanted him to ask. "Blow jobs don't count," I said. "You could have at least taken pictures," he said. "You could have at least written." He took his belt out, and his pants fell to the floor. "The mailman avoids me."

I went for a walk. When I came back, he had pulled all the books off my shelves and made two piles. "This pile is true," he said, pointing to the far smaller pile. "And this pile," he said, shaking, "is lies." His grin was screwed on wrong. I saw different teeth in it. His sex was pointed at me.

"So?" I said, grabbing him by it. "So what?"

"We are going to fuck now."

It was our last time, and it didn't last long, but at least I came. We were both pretty worked up.

But we were also hungry and needed a drink, so afterward we went out for a change. I chose an unself-consciously ratty bistro in Pigalle. At the table next to ours sat two men, one older and gray as ash, the other young and black. They leaned over and talked to me while Eli drank carafe after carafe of house rouge and listened for words that sounded sexy or mean, at which point he'd butt in, but in French that's like looking for a certain needle in a stack of needles. One and a half carafes of wine later, Eli asked, "What's French for 'fuck'?" I could tell by looking at him that he was trying not to see double and, for the time being, more or less succeeding. I could also feel him slipping away. There were two of him now, and they were both slipping away.

The black guy looked at Eli and said, almost without accent, "It depends. What kind of fucking?" Then to his friend and me he said, *"Bah, alors, ça explique tout! Les Amerloques ils ont qu'un seul mot pour dire baisser."*

"Come again?" Eli said, squinting as if the sun were in his eyes.

"I said, you Americans are puerile—all you think about is fucking and yet have just one word for it."

Eli told him we've got plenty of terms, like hate fucking. And regular fucking. And stuff. And everybody laughed except for Eli, who just flagged down the *garçon* for some brandy. Calvados, *Hors d'Age.* "Tell your friend," the black man told me in French, "that we would both very much like to fuck him." I felt hot. "You could watch, of course," he added when I didn't respond right away. But by the time I leaned over to pass the message along to Eli, he was gone.

"Where did he go?" I asked them in French.

"Il s'est cassé," the black guy said, shrugging. "Just fucked off. Pity."

I threw down way more francs than our meal could've possibly cost and ran out onto the street. The waiter yelled after me. *"C'est là. C'est là! Tout est là!"* I yelled back. The drinks, I remembered. We had a *lot* of drinks. I felt inclines where there were none. The waiter's *mademoiselles* turned into *salopes*. But in France, cursing is the sound of someone giving up. So I slowed down. Then I heard thin soles slapping against sidewalk. He grabbed my arm just above the elbow. *"Regardez!"* he said, shoving the *billet* into the side of my face. *"Vous me devez quarante francs!"*

"Ça va, ça va," I said, reaching into my purse and pulling out a fifty. *"Putain! Voilà!"*

He let go of me with a little push. I stumbled into a *bitte*, which I then used to straighten up. "Cunt," he said. I spat more or less at his feet, missing him by a good foot or two. The waiter looked down at his shoes, and Eli flew out of nowhere and straight into the wall between us. *"Mais, vous êtes completement fous,"* the waiter yelled at Eli's heap, shuffling backwards. *"Ça va pas la tête!"*

Eli got up and smiled blood at him. "No," he said. *"Ça va pas."*

The waiter turned and ran, and Eli chased after him. "I'll show you cunt!" Eli yelled. "Look, you dick!" Eli stopped long enough to punch himself in the face and tear at his hair. Then he took off down the street.

I took a deep breath—leaded gas, sewer, creosote—and followed them.

Two streets over, past the bistro, the waiter had lost us. Eli teetered blank-faced over a man who bent stolen café forks into gargoyles. "Look," he said, shaking. "Demons."

The man bent a tine into a snake tongue. "I don't want to always help you," I said to Eli, turning to leave.

"Wait," he said. And then, a little too clearly—as though he had suddenly come to, which he hadn't—he said, "Do you think I need you?"

"Fuck you," I got out. Eli just looked at me with what I think I now know to be confusion. It was a question after all, not a point he was trying to make, and I had somehow forgotten that Eli never asked questions that he knew the answer to. In class, he always wanted us to talk among ourselves, but our conversations never went anywhere without him at their center. *"You don't need me,"* he would shout, pulling on his tie. *"Go on! Talk! For christsake, talk! Talk, you babies."*

"I helped you. I might've even saved your life," he said, falling into the shuttered shopfront window of what couldn't have possibly been that ratcatcher's or the taxidermist's. It wasn't a movie, so it was just some shop that neither mattered nor meant anything.

I turned my back and walked toward home.

"We can take turns," he shouted. "We'll try!"

I tried not to weave and in all likelihood failed. Eli was somewhere behind me. He didn't look as small as I'd hoped he'd look in Paris. If anything, he looked bigger. I went down into the Metro. Stamped my ticket, walked onto the platform. Eli, meanwhile, fumbled through his many pockets, looking for his *carnet*, yelling at his pockets and at me. "Now see here," he yelled. The train pulled up. There had been some kind of match, or strike, and the car was oddly full and loud for that time of night. The doors opened, and someone pulled me in. The doors closed in Eli's red face. A transport cop grabbed his arm, and we were sucked into the tunnel, the whole car cheering.

I spent that night and the next seven nights at a girlfriend's in La Défense. I didn't go to class. Eli had no idea where to look for me. His flight was in a week. When I went back to my place, there was a clean spot on the floor where he had slept outside my door and a neat little stack of bottle caps. I had missed my chance to say goodbye.

Georgie was out front, wiping down a car with a dirty rag. He stopped when he saw me. I pretended not to see him, but pretending not see someone doesn't work with guys like Georgie.

"Hey!"

Same with pretending you haven't heard them.

"I just want to show you something." He walked toward me.

I turned back around. "You can tell me from there."

"I can't tell you nothing. This is something I got to show you."

"What."

"Just come here. You gotta take a look at this."

"Leave me alone."

"Ah, c'mon."

"No, I'm asking you: If I look at this one thing, will you leave me alone? From now on?"

"Sure," he said.

"Okay," I said, and walked toward him. The sun was low, and we were both being loud: me on purpose, him because he couldn't help it. I approached him, and he stepped aside, giving me a path and pointing at the car parked facing the wrong way right in front of the club. He pointed at the driver's side-view. "That mirror. How come it don't got that warning about things looking smaller in them. Other side's got one."

"Maybe it's a mistake."

"They don't make mistakes like that at a factory. I worked in a factory, okay. There's spics lined up around the block waiting to take your job for half what you make. That shit happens on purpose."

"Maybe they thought it would distract the driver. Like he should know how side-views work if he's behind the wheel. Like he should already know from mirrors."

"That's a good answer."

"Are we through?" I started walking backwards. "'Cause I need to pick up my boyfriend, he's gonna be ho—"

"He's dead."

I stopped, thinking he meant my boyfriend, thinking that meant Eli. I felt nineteen all of a sudden. "What?"

"They found them, he's dead."

"Who's dead?"

"That guy."

"What *guy*?" I started walking backward again, toward something that might have been my car.

"That guy that looks like a dinosaur."

"Huh." I stopped.

"Yeah. He washed up on the shore of that lake where he lives. Read it in the paper."

"The paper." I looked over my shoulder. There were no cars. No people to see. No one to help.

"I believe in all that shit: ghosts, dinosaurs." The whole street was quiet. "Jesus." He stepped closer. "I was an instrument baby."

"Oh," I said.

"Got caught inside my mom. They used howyoucallit—clamps—to get me out. You can see the marks." He leaned into the security light outside the club and pointed at the dent in the left side of his forehead. "Killed my mother, though."

"I'm sorry."

"Not your fault."

"Okay. Bye."

"Come on, Alix, that's not how to be a neighbor."

"I mean it. About my name, about everything. Leave me alone." I put my hand out, as if I were blocking a spell. He stopped and stared at me, his mouth open.

I got in my car and peeled out. By the time I crossed downtown, I realized that I knew where I was going all along.

I'd heard that Eli was living on Ives Street, at the corner of Transit. There was no doorbell, so I knocked on the blinded window nearest the front door until a black-pored nose poked through the slats. Then an eye, which squinted, then widened and disappeared behind rattling blinds. Then something fell. Keys. At least a minute's worth of quiet. It had been so long, and I had heard so many things, that I didn't know what to expect. The deadbolt clicked and there he was: older and thinner, as gray and pitted as concrete.

It took longer than it should have for me to realize he was also shirtless. Eli used to avoid pointless shirtlessness—hated his hairless chest, his inverted left nipple, and, depending on the light, the briefest shadow of breasts. But now his torso was simultaneously withered and sinewy, and it looked like he had grown hair at some point but that most of it had fallen out. Like a bomb had gone off in him. He'd also grown two extra nipples—one red, the other clear—and all four of them were hard.

I realized I was staring, but he had the kind of eyes where you couldn't tell if he was staring or not, so I don't know if he saw me. I also realized that I hadn't said anything yet, so I said hi and his name. He said nothing, but made a noise that might have been a word or words. Then he coughed and lit a cigarette and pinched it out and put it behind his ear.

"Why are you come," he said, wincing.

I winced, too. "It's been a while." Which was true, but not an answer.

"Yeah. And stuff." He took a different half-smoked cigarette out of his back pocket and lit it.

"Can I come in?"

He took a deep drag and held it like it was the pot he probably would've rather been smoking at that exact moment. He shook his head like he didn't know what I was talking about, but not in an evasive way—like he literally couldn't understand the question. He kept on holding his breath and shaking his head. Smoke fell then rose from his nostrils. Behind us, a German car was turning onto Ives. My skin tightened.

"Look, Eli. I don't want to stand here."

He held the door for me in such a way that I had to duck under his arm and contort so as not to brush against his crotch. He smelled just how you'd expect a shirtless, chain-smoking yard worker on the wrong side of thirty to smell. No better, no worse. So there was that at least.

His apartment was an efficiency and seemingly empty but for a table and two chairs, which also gave me hope, until I realized that they matched the cabinets. He sat down in one with a blanket folded over its back and gestured at the empty one with his cigarette. Then he ashed into the quahog shell now wobbling between us. The apartment smelled like his scalp. I looked around, stealing a quick glimpse into his bedroom, empty except for a straight-backed chair and something small and gray beside it.

He noticed me noticing this. "I—uh—I'm thinking of sleeping in the kitchen," he said.

"Oh yeah?" It looked like he'd been doing so for some time.

"Yeah. In my bedroom, just a chair. To sit in." He put out his Camel and pulled out a pouch of Three Castles and rolled himself one. "I'll look out the window, when I get home. There's a tree the moths didn't get."

"Sounds nice." There were only gaps between what few practical items his apartment contained: a box of matches, a can of coffee, some grain in a jar. It was tidy, but how could it not be? There was work grit in the corners and a broom leaning against the wall.

"After work," he said.

"Sometimes sitting helps."

"And stuff."

"Look, Eli—" I started. Eli hugged his left arm to his side and rocked a little in his chair, which squeaked as he rocked. Smoke rose around him like fog. No, like smoke. Like the cigarette smoke it was. I uncrossed and recrossed my legs under the table, kicking something on the floor. Eli was still angled toward the bedroom, so I glanced down and saw a fingerprinty sneaker box, with an almost completely faded blue Tretorn loop. My heart did something, then did its opposite twice as fast. With the toe of my shoe I tipped open the lid, and there they were: the black-and-whites Viv had taken of us, now wrapped in milky-looking paper. As far as I could tell, the corners weren't so much as kinked. My throat caught and my eyes filled up, but what did it matter. Eli couldn't look at me. I replaced the lid with my foot. "Eli," I said.

He stopped rocking.

"Did—I just want to . . . I mean, I want to know—" I stopped myself. And we both stayed quiet and still long enough for me to become aware of the sound of his apartment, a low, minor hum. I picked up the box and put it on the table between us. Eli looked at it, then at me, then quickly looked away.

"This is mine," I said.

He shut his eyes and cocked his head to the right. "There was stuff I wanted to tell you," he said, his eyes still closed. "But my head hurts."

And I thinned my lips together and nodded at him. We sat there silently, Eli sneaking awkward red-eyed peeks at me and at the box until the apartment hum changed keys.

I pushed out my chair and picked up the box, but a long, invisible pin pierced my wrist and I dropped it. The sound made my ears ring. Black-and-whites were scattered across the linoleum floor as if they'd been arranged by someone who wanted to re-create an accident in a film or in a museum. I saw a knee—my knee. My hair. My navel.

Quickly gathered up, they looked like pictures of someone else. Eli got down on the floor with me, his belly flesh folded into deckles, and picked the photos up by the edges, one by one, with his fingertips. Together we returned them all to the box, to the crinkly white paper. He folded the paper over. I closed the lid. Using my forearms more than my hands, I put the box back under the table.

"Goodbye, Eli," I said, and meant it—really really did. I thought the word itself might help, which isn't like me, and of course it didn't. But maybe it didn't hurt, either? I have to believe it didn't. Good luck, I only thought, and saw myself out.

It was an hour before family meal. If I could find a pay phone, I could maybe still get someone to cover my shift.

(......)

I: ALIX AND I MET THE DAY WE—ME AND MY SISTER—BURIED ELI, meaning put his ashes in a box and sent them home with Libby. I made sure to focus on the space between Alix's eyes while we talked, a trick an otherwise useless alienist had taught me. She excused herself pretty abruptly. Either Eli had warned her—a convenient little bit of self-flattery that would've been like him back then; I can just hear him blackening my name—or else she could see right through me on her own. But before she hugged Libby—who didn't blame *her* for all of this—and left, she did tell me that Eli wrote a note. He mailed it to her along with that shoebox and all its contents:

Can't see myself working tomorrow.

That's it.

Back-to-back Expository classes: According to the URI English Department website, Alix's two Intro Expository sections are now being covered by a visiting professor of Fan Fiction.

Eviction: On the morning of October 14, 1999, at seven sharp, the twenty-seven inhabitants of the third and fourth floors of One Eagle Square were forcibly removed from their commercially zoned domiciles by the Providence fire and police departments, the property having been, just the week prior, purchased by Sanderson & Sons, who planned on turning the entire complex into a luxury mixed-use condominium.*

> *The Baltimore-based company's lawyer immediately procured a Historical Society–approved tax credit for this development, and his clients would pay only a tenth of the assessed taxes for the next ten years. Given the area's superficial similarity to industrial Brooklyn, Sanderson & Sons had sold the city on a build-to-suit Olneyville built just for suits. But the question of where exactly these new residents—childless academics? gay internists? Korean architecture students?—would earn their above-market rents went unasked, and even well before the Big Fire* the project was considered a misstep akin to the city's puzzling mid-'60s decision to pave over the confluence of the Moshassuck and Woonasquatucket Rivers with what few people realized wasn't any old rotary, but, in fact, the world's widest bridge. Locals called it Suicide Circle. It was our best joke.
>
>> *On May 11, 2001, the newly renovated and still-unoccupied Eagle Mills was burned to the ground by an as-yet unidentified arsonist. Whispers persist that its main investors were already looking for an out. Rhode Islanders, as you might imagine, tend to suspect kike lightning whenever old buildings go up in smoke. But despite my self-loathing and my oft-circuitous methods of graphing history's enfoldments, I firmly believe that horses and zebras alike will take the shortest, straightest

route between two points, unless of course they are being shot at from multiple angles.* In the end, the reader must reach her own conclusions.

*As a college sophomore, I enrolled myself in Kermit Barker's popular Quantum Uncertainty—referred to around campus as Physics for Sickos. Dr. Barker was beloved and pitied for having suffered a protracted nervous breakdown first spurred on by mid-twentieth-century breakthroughs in the field to which he had already dedicated more than half his life. Like so many Depression-born and -prone physicists, he suddenly discovered that damn near everything he had been taught and had thought up until then was *not* "true." At least not observably. Not dependably. Not *scientifically*. He made it his life's work to pass this awesome disillusionment on to his students in a manner that managed to be both theatrical and sincere: "We don't know what happens to it," he'd say in response to just about any question regarding ostensibly observable subatomic phenomena. "We don't know! All we know is that watching it changes things. It could turn into a rhinoceros! Two pickles! A lady—or her hat! We can't know . . ." He would then burst into very real, very observable tears and flee the auditorium. At least once a semester he broke down and gave everyone either A's or F's, and, one year, elephants.

My baby brother's going to prison: A public show of support for Kit's brother from former governor Jordan Falleman* helped little: "Fud is one of us," he wrote in an open letter. "He is a brother, a friend, and a sailor."

*The same Falleman who would nip my public notary business in the bud a mere six weeks in. But I knew it was coming. After setting up my cot and a hot plate in the office's backroom and scrubbing the WC sink clean with a toothbrush and a can of Clabber Girl, I discovered that, according to Section 11 of *Standards of Conduct for Notaries Public in the State of Rhode Island and Providence Plantations*, an NP may, at any time and for any reason, "be removed . . . by the Governor, in his or her discretion." Two years earlier, you see, I had caught His Honor, half in the bag by six, hectoring a supermarket cashier over the price of herring snacks, so I told him to give the poor kid a break, he didn't write the circular, and, when that didn't work, to go fuck himself, at which point he knocked the hat from my head. A stock boy jumped between us, but not before I had shoved my calling card* into the breast pocket of the governor's topcoat. "I demand satisfaction," I yelled as the stock boy dragged me out of the store. Over everybody's head, the cashier shot me two quick thumbs-ups. Later I returned to collect my Bactine and my hat, still sitting there, on the checkout aisle floor beneath the gum.

*It read, simply:

CLAY BLACKALL

Knowledgeable in Some Matters

Tampon incident: My knowledge of exactly what transpired that Indian-summery afternoon remains limited. (Events now known within an increasingly less tight but ever smaller circle as the other "other 9/11.") So I will leave the reenvisioning of these events to Vivian Goddard (*see her "Neoteny"*).

... abandoned tenements that dead-ended near the foot of the Prospect Park wall: My grandpa Ike's properties.* I know it's hard now to imagine so forlorn a block on College Hill, but in some respects Providence has changed. On the surface, at least. The three triple-deckers sat side by each, shaded by the statue of the state founder, Roger Williams,** patting with his (own) foot-size hand the head of an invisible indigenous boy long since removed thanks to increased public sensitivity to scale and/or race. By this point, the houses had been sitting unoccupied for at least a decade. After some twenty-odd years of renting to students, Ike had decided enough was enough. "You should see these places in June! They're worse than drug addicts, these college kids! Let that painted baboon Gorman clean up after 'em. I'm done." While waiting for a fire or another RISD expansion, Ike focused instead on Mount Hope and Smith Hill, where he knew what to expect and what to look for.

*Shortly after Grandma Tillie's death, Grandpa Ike sold his remaining tenements to his longtime property manager, Frank Luongo (*see "Side by Each"*), and moved to West Boca. "Look, I'm a Jew," Ike told me. "What do I need from old houses and snow? We got the past in our guts and cold in our joints." I didn't respond, so he said, "I don't have another funeral in me," and that was the end of that.

**It marks what little remains of the great man's remains. In preparation for the big reburial, Williams's coffin was exhumed from the basement of his home and discovered to hold nothing but some dirt and the taproot of an apple tree. After much hand-wringing, these contents were moved, placed in a granite tomb, and buried beneath the above-mentioned statue. What became of the corpse no one can say, but many theories of varying plausibility abound, most of which cast aspersions on Anne Hutchinson, banished from the Massachusetts Bay Colony for antinomian heresy and now all too often referred to as Roger Williams's "witch girlfriend."*

> *Why do we still want so badly to believe in witches? And to blame them when things don't turn out the way we'd hoped? Eli used to argue that *Plastic Ono Band* was Lennon's best work,* and I agree.
>
> > *But he also used to pretend that the Beatles were the Monks whenever anyone else brought them up. And he would never let it go, would pretend not to understand their confusion and, eventually, their anger. "I love 'I Hate You' best," he would say. "Stop it!" they would shout. "Yes!" he would say. "And how about that 'Cuckoo'? Wow. Oh, wow!"*
> >
> > > *I can't believe I almost forgot about this! There's something around every corner, under every rock. I get in my own way a lot, but I can't stop looking.

My father—who I called Ned: Ned Dubberford, Fox's headmaster.

My idiot brother's expulsion: My Fox classmate, Teddy "Cree" Dubberford. Young Teddy had got himself kicked out of Fox* for jumping off a moving school bus on the way home from Fall Fun

Fest. But little did Ned or anyone else know, Teddy made the leap only because his briefs had, mere seconds earlier, filled up with what felt like a quart of come. At the rear of the bus—one row in from the emergency exit—sophomore Gina McQueen, scandalously clad in a bikini top and what were supposed to be shorts, had been playing a playful game of catch with Teddy across the aisle until he caught the glimpse that broke the camel's hump. Teddy then leaped from his seat—a jacket held fast to his lap—and emergency-exited the moving bus. While his classmates whistled and cheered, Teddy's still-bent legs—remember, he had that hard-on to hide!—folded up under him like a card table's and he hit the ground chin-first. Full of adrenaline, Teddy spat some teeth, picked himself up, and made straight for the woods, where he hid till dark.

*On its own, such a stunt wouldn't have been enough to earn the headmaster's son anything more than a stern talking-to. Not in the late '70s. Not at Fox, at any rate. But since Teddy had already been caught covering his English teacher's Dodge first with pineapple rings, then papier-mâché pricks, and, last of all, a mock cherry felled during the spring musical (a toothless *Pippin*) while he was supposed to have been running lights, his father was left with no choice but to send his eldest packing for an alternative correctional institution in the foothills of the White Mountains.* His family all took turns shaking his hand and wishing him luck—except for Alix, who stayed home, listening to Blondie and reading Judy Blume or doing whatever it is nine-year-old girls did in 1980 when having none of it.

*Zeno's Zen Archery Academy, in craggy Aporia Falls. Cree has since returned to Providence and was recently arrested for hiding a camera in the unisex bathroom at the Wickenden Street café where he worked. Over the

> course of six years he filmed a healthy cross section of the city's residents in various states of undress and relief. It all came to a head when a peeing Brown coed leaned down to retrieve a dropped cell phone and spied an electric eye duct-taped beneath the sink, staring unblinkingly at her bare lap. She ripped the whole setup out and dropped it on the counter by way of asking what the fuck. *I mean, what the fuck?* It didn't take long to figure out who had set it up, given that Cree had—inadvertently—filmed himself doing exactly that at the tape's start. His name and address were published in the next morning's paper. Meanwhile, Cree hides in plain sight. His trial date looms, and those still close to him say he hardly seems himself.

Secretary: That same Gina McQueen. She obviously made a pretty big impression on Pops, too. As for how Teddy took all this, I'd say not well. Not well at all.

. . . Lovecraft's grave: Practically spitting distance from my room at Butler—and I would know, as during my brief stay there I did a power of spitting. Granted, I've never been on a date; nevertheless, Eli's tour strikes me as overdetermined—the sort led by a guy in period garb who discourages slowpokery but can't read faces. Why, the only thing missing is a quick pit stop at the Industrial Trust building, which delusional locals insist on thinking of as the *Daily Planet* from the old Superman serial.

Eli took a job at the Borders in Cranston: Where he edited the store's newsletter. In his first and last issue, Eli introduced his short-lived alter ego, Cleats McNeil, a crazy-legged and leather-helmeted varsity end who crashed weekly his rumble-seated sawbuck-green roadster. My brother then went on to offer kudos to the café on the pine-flavored coffee, and to pine for a lady friend of his very own—someone who wouldn't get all sore at him if he broke the horns off her unicorns or the wings from her Pegasuses or peg legs off her pirates or show him the door for drinking from the finger bowl. I didn't think to hold on to my copy, which Eli had, uncharacteristically, slipped through my mail slot. He was proud, I guess. It seems I've held on to all the wrong things over the years.

"Tell your friend we would like to fuck him": Eli told me that the closest he'd ever come was a two-dude three-way. We both made faces. "Like sharing an armrest," he told me. "And you both need the ashtray." But that was just him trying to make me jealous. He was always finding new ways. Words could split me in two, and he knew it. Names have always hurt me.

Louder Than Good

Cliff Hinson

Rob and I found the secret room after seeing a movie with explosions and ghosts in it. It was the first time either of us had ever set foot in the mall. We weren't going out of our way to avoid the place, even though it was built by the exact same dicks who bought Eagle Square out from under us. It's just, it's the mall.

We caught the midnight show, so by the time it let out, the stores were closed and the lights were all half off. People on the down escalator stared straight ahead, already in their cars in their minds. Rob and I took the stairs. Flight after flight, we kept going down, looking at each other, thinking, this can't be right, can it? How many stories is this place? Five at least. Felt like eight. You could smell the river: copper, feces, geese. Something was humming. The hum got louder. The handrails were vibrating, and we hadn't seen an exit sign in at least three flights.

The door to the subbasement crash-barred open onto a long corridor, lit only by red alarm lights. Our footsteps hardly echoed. At the corridor's end an extra-large Dunkin' Donuts travel mug propped open a door with no handle. I pulled the door all the way open, and Rob felt around for the lights. They flickered onto a raw concrete room, roughly twenty by twenty, with ten-foot ceilings. The far right corner was wet, but opposite it was a couch scattered all around with lunch-break detritus: coffee cups, cigarette butts, beer cans, stroke books. Judging from all the dust and the dates on the sports sections, no one had been in the room since spring of '97, which is when the mall was finished. This couldn't have been a coincidence. Our footprints were the only ones in the dust. We looked around and then at each other's idea-lightbulbs and laughed.

Later, from a pay phone down the street, we called Pete-Peter, who said right-on and he'd tell Andyman, because you never know with Andyman. It was a couple months after the eviction, and we were crashing here and there, holding out for someplace big and cheap where we could fuck up the floors and make all the noise we wanted.

The pay phone looked out on what was going to be a luxury condo but for now was just a diner-shaped hole. Rob had worked at that diner for a minute in the early '90s. In fact, it's where we first met, when he served me a cup of coffee with his thumb in it. I asked him if it hurt, and he grinned at me like we were in this together. His teeth were crooked like mine. I miss their corned beef hash, which didn't taste homemade but was.

We moved into the secret room piecemeal, stuffing what little we needed into duffel bags and making trips a couple-two-three times a day under cover of the busiest business hours. We brought some pots and pans, a hot plate, milk crates, clothes, a stereo. There was also what was left of our old space. The building's new owners figured it was garbage, so they hadn't thrown it out. It took a whole lot of trips to get the caftan maze down there, and the wall's worth of action figure torsos. My hips started to hurt from all the up and down, but that's because we're meant to live in trees.

Between Fire & Ice and the Melting Pot, the Dumpster provided us with more than enough root ends and peels and ugly bits for the stockpot, which, because of the free electricity, was pretty much always simmering. In it we cooked beans and grains and other cheap, dry items. We would come and go when we pleased, and when the weather was nice, didn't spend that much time down there.

We got invited over friends' places for showers and sleepovers. Before long, Andyman took off for a family cabin in Maine or Vermont or wherever. I saw less and less of Pete-Peter, who'd met a girl and got a job fixing bikes. Me, I hung out more and more and drew on the walls. I drew friends mostly, doing different things. Viv with a tricorne and a musket. Andyman sticking Sanderson and Sons' heads on pikes. Rob in a diaper. Rob in a pelt, brandishing a club. I drew the rooster I had given him years back that thought dawn came every hour until Rob made soup out of him. I drew an outline of Rhode Island with a thirteen in it. I crossed out the thirteen with a calumet. "WHAT CHEER!" I wrote. "WITNESS THE WORLD'S CRAZIEST PILGRIM!" I drew a sun smoking.

More and more, Rob would show up just to crash and be either gone or asleep by the time I'd wake up. Nights, I'd wait up for him and leave a light on and the door propped open before I went to bed. I'd sing "Keep Your Lamps Trimmed and Burning" to keep myself company. I'd hear things—crackles, bumps, concrete scraping. At night my spine would prickle. Spooked, I sat with my back against the wall until the cold and the damp seeping through it gave me chicken skin. I knitted myself a cape from maze scraps and left it on while I drew, read, ate soup.

One morning Rob showed up looking at least as bad as he felt. It took me a minute to recognize him. It had been a bunch of weeks at this point. I turned on the lights, and he covered his eyes.

"I'm going to kick," he said.

"Okay," I said. "I can help."

"No you can't."

"I'm right here."

"It gets loud in my head," Rob told me, pointing crookedly at his temple.

"We'll make something," I said.

"I'm in no kind of shape."

"After, then. We've got time."

"Yeah," he said, hugging himself.

"Promise," I said, covering him.

"Fuck you," he said.

"Promise, you son of a bitch."

"Once I feel better," he said, uncovering himself.

"Life is not how you feel, asshole." I was going to add that life is not what you want, either, but I took a good, long look at him, shivering hot like that, feeling the two months' worth of pain he had created and put off, then redoubled and decided against it. He pulled the blanket back up and kicked it off again and vomited into the first thing he grabbed—a hat Alix never wore and left behind that Rob had kept.

"You good for an hour?" I asked.

"Fuck you. This is my idea," he said, pulling the blanket back up.

"Okay," I said, and left, leaving the door propped.

I showed up an hour later with a couple bags of groceries and a stack of paperbacks about the future.

For the next three days I drew marks on the wall to represent those days. "You remember jail, right?" I said.

"You mean prison," he said. "And fuck you."

I cleaned up his vomit. I threw out his shitted sheets. I called him asshole and fucking prick to encourage him. One time I kneeled on his chest. Later I put alcohol on the spots where his nails broke my skin.

By the time Rob had sweated his way through it, I finally gave in to the flu that I had been staving off. My flu looked and smelled almost exactly like his cold turkey, right down to the sick boners, which don't make any fucking sense at all.

Once I could keep my liquids down, we spent another week or so in fake lockdown, a week during which we were well enough to read, but not to think or make anything, so we tore through the books. We liked them okay. Me more than him. But he'd already reread all his own books too many times—Philip K. Dick, mostly, but also Nietzsche and someone Russian or something—so passing the time was enough.

When we were both more or less back to normal, I went upstairs to grab refreshments at the CVS that had replaced the toy store. But first I asked for some money, and, like a dick, Rob made me turn around while he extracted a locked metal box from its hiding spot. But I only heard change. "You miser," I said. "No wonder you started using again. You gotta work less."

"Fuck you, hippy," he said, handing me three bucks' worth of coins—buffalo nickels mostly, but also oddball dimes and one of those Bicentennials—and a two-dollar bill for the paper and some Cup-a-Soups and whatever else.

"You're like a crazy old lady, all holed up with rare denominations. What else you got hidden?"

Rob's middle finger was long and straight, and he never bothered with knuckle balls, which somehow made it even worse.

We didn't make the Cup-a-Soups, but in the Lifebeat! section of the paper I saw a notice for a traveling exhibition of Chernobyl photographs at the Ukrainian Social Club in Pawtucket. We hadn't even known there was a Ukrainian Club in Pawtucket, but it was the last day, so we went.

The photos were exactly as amazing and awful as you'd expect. Red walls looked green, and the green desks were rusted red. Paint peeled from buildings like burnt skin. What, from across the room, appeared to be a gray mound of stomachs turned out to be abandoned gas masks. The lenses were covered in ash. Trees grew through cars, buildings, other trees. Basically extinct horses ate grass. Mushrooms looked like cartoon mushrooms: swollen, red-capped, deadly. Cranes and wolves and boars frolicked and hunted like humans had never existed, their insides burning with radiation. I took off my sweatshirt, put it back on, took it off again, wiped my face with it. I couldn't swallow. An electric sizzle traveled from my jaw to my eye. My eye started twitching.

Rob put his sunglasses back on. We nodded at each other and were about to walk out when we saw this beautiful white cake sitting on a table, beside which stood two old ladies in calf-length skirt suits. The cake had three layers at least and was completely, perfectly white. So white it looked almost black. Like a big blank wedding cake. You could see anything you wanted to in it. There were two pieces missing, or maybe just one big slice, and we hadn't eaten anything in a long time. Rob took off his sunglasses. "That's a beautiful cake," he said, smiling. For Rob, charm was something you do, not something you have, and it worked.

"That's His Excellency's cake," the older of the two ladies said, getting taller.

"His Excellency?" Rob said, cocking his head to the left a bit.

"The Ukrainian ambassador. He was here this morning."

"Did he like the cake?"

"He declared it . . . *exquisite*," she said, taking her time with the word, which, with her accent, sounded like actual sex on her lips.

"*Exquisite*," Rob repeated.

"Yes, *exquisite*," she said one more time, disappearing into her own mind for a moment. "Would you like a slice?" she asked, remembering herself. She picked up the cake server, which was also a knife. We said yes, thank you, *of course we would*, and ate the cake on the steps of the club, squinting into the sun. It tasted even whiter than it looked. It was dense and sweet, and you noticed what you didn't taste. It tasted like metal, almost. We hadn't eaten in weeks.

We offered to rinse our plates, after, but of course they wouldn't hear of it.

By early fall, Rob was crashing with Alix again. "We're giving it another shot," he said, kicking a chunk of concrete into a pothole.

We were standing in the parking lot of a Cambodian restaurant. Rob's face was still red from all the pickled peppers I'd dared him to eat. Either way, lunch was on him.

He was mostly pointed away from me, and he kept shifting his weight like he had somewhere to be. His pupils were small, but it was sunny out. I didn't even really know what to look for.

"Alix is the best," I said.

Rob made that fucking teenage cowboy face I fucking hate.

"Asshole," I said. "I'm rooting for both of you here."

"We're not a team," he said.

"We're all in this together," I said.

I gave Rob and Alix a month, two tops. But who cares. I only knew I would be there for him when it fell through, because what else are you gonna do?

And now, a year after we found it, the secret room was just where I lived. People stopped by to visit, to smoke weed, to see it for themselves. "You live in the mall!" they'd say. I'd say, did you know the guys who built the parking garage won't park in it? A place doesn't have to be old to be history.

They mostly told me more and worse things about Rob. That he and Alix were through. He wouldn't go out without sunglasses on. He no longer slept or ate. He'd taken a caretaker's job to avoid people entirely. The Lyme he caught living on that yurt on Despair Island had finally gotten to his brain. He started using again. Probably. I mean, what else could he be doing out there, they said. His teeth had fallen out and his hands were like oven mitts. All of them—a few of whom Rob didn't know and an even fewer of whom

Rob even liked—were really worried. Someone else said he was in the pokey. They even used that word, *pokey*, which threw me for a minute. "Jail," they said, misreading my confusion.

"Prison, you mean," I said.

Meanwhile, the night watchman's shoes made small, hoof-like noises in the stairs and halls. He made his rounds above me, looking for places to hide from the cameras. The secret room would hold a certain appeal for a man like that. But it felt like I had imagined him into existence. I stayed put and he kept descending deeper and deeper into the mall. Before long, I lost track of the days. And sure enough, late one night, the door creaked open and a flashlight hit me on the couch, eating hominy from a mixing bowl with a wooden spoon. "What?" he said. "Who are you? How did you get in here?"

"I'm a ghost," I said, thinking about it. "And I'm a ghost."

"You—you can't be here. This is a mall."

"I don't even know what that means."

"It means you're trespassing," he said, shaking his flashlight beam all around the room, at the table and the hot plate and the bedrolls, all the time feeling around his hip for something that wasn't there. A gun? I'm not sure he had ever worn a gun. "Jesus," he said. "How many of there are you?"

"Can't you see?"

"I see you."

"There's more. There's two of us."

"I'm going to call this in," he said, fumbling for his walkie-talkie. "There will be backup. Police."

"You don't need to do this," I said.

"You are breaking the law just being here."

"You are choosing to do this. This is a choice you are doing."

"This is my job."

"Exactly."

"I'm calling it in."

So I got up, put the mixing bowl down on the couch, and walked toward the door.

"You're not going anywhere," he said, trying to block me in.

But I kept walking toward him. When I got close enough, I hugged him and hugged him over to one side and said into his ear, which smelled like an ear, "You are not a job." I said it twice, maybe three times, at which point he stopped struggling and I let him go. I walked through the door, moving neither quickly nor slowly down the hallway. My back felt giant, tight. He didn't come after me. He did call it in, but by the time the cars pulled up, I was walking along the Woonasquatucket in the dark and keeping an eye out for wild animals, which are everywhere if you look for them, like marbles and buttons. I find buttons all the time. My pockets rattle.

Pete-Peter moved in with his girlfriend, who looks exactly like him, only smaller and prettier and a little sadder, maybe. Sleepy put Manchild back together and hit the road for gas money and performance-space meals and floors to sleep on. And at some point Pete-Peter had started hanging out with the new kids.

I figured I could crash at what was now just Alix's for a while. She had room. So I biked over to Carpenter on my tandem, which I kept chained to the guardrail underneath some brush at the far end of Harris. I took the long way around to avoid hills. The bike listed from side to side while I pedaled, as heavy as a length of scaffold. I wobbled down streets and weaved around corners.

When I got to what had been their place, I knocked and knocked, but there was no answer. The blinds were all down. I knocked again. I knocked and I knocked and knocked some more.

I'm pretty good at breaking into houses on account of being a latchkey kid who lost his keys a lot. But I figured I'd just rest a bit and wait. I sat down on the stoop and leaned against the door until it opened up behind me and I fell into a big pile of mail: junk mostly—circulars and rental center coupons—but also some bills.

Two, three weeks of mail, at least. It wasn't like either of them to leave their door unlocked, so I got up and walked up the stairs and into the apartment, calling her name and Rob's name, just to be sure, and eventually alternating between them, with a pause that got longer, then shorter. Then I realized what I was doing and stopped and just poked around. They didn't own much, and Rob had left most of his birds and things back at Eagle Square. There was their shitty furniture. Rob's books and what was left of his records. Some condiments in the kitchen. The refrigerator door was open, and the lights didn't work. But something stank, literally. And not in the kitchen. I followed the smell.

What Alix had begun cultivating a couple years back wasn't really a mushroom—it was a bacterial colony—but that's what she called the gray, waxy-looking thing now living in a rag-covered dish beside the radiator. Thinking mostly about getting rid of the smell, I grabbed the mushroom and carried it out with me, making sure to lock the door.

The night was quiet and damp. Waves of streetlight-lit mist rose up out of the gutters and through grates. I lowered the mushroom dish into the milk box welded to the front of the tandem and swaddled it with my sweatshirt to secure it. Every time I hit a pothole, the milk box lid jumped, releasing sour fumes. As I turned onto Broadway, the lid yawned open long enough to make me cough vomit. I spat and headed southeast toward the bike path. With the tandem, I figured I'd be better off biking through the night.

Once I got to Jamestown, the sky was dishwatery, and I realized I had no way of contacting Rob because of course there was no phone. But there the house on the rock was, and there he was, maybe. I jumped up and down on the beach a little, yelling and trying to get his attention, but that didn't work. It was close, the rock, but not close enough. I scoured the banks for something louder than my voice and, like a miracle, found a barnacled length of PVC pipe. I put my lips to one end and fucking laid into it. I blew like I was calling up ghosts. I blew and blew till my head went white and I had no breath left in any part of my body, not even my feet. At some point the beach turned white also, then shrank and took a swing at me, so I sat down on a rock until the color came back. Then I ditched the tandem in some bushes and grabbed the mushroom, sloshing and oozing and oddly hot inside its milk-glass pot, and carried it over to the dock, where I saw a guy who'd already been having a conversation with me for who knows how long. "And this man who lived in the room before me," he said pointing over my shoulder in the direction of something, "was Buckminster Fuller!"

"Listen," I said. "Can you give me a ride out to that house."

"Where's the safest place to be in a storm?"

"Where?" I asked.

"The open ocean!"

"No shit?"

"Climb in," he said. He handed me a thermos. "Have some coffee."

In the boat, over the outboard's whine, I drank hot black coffee while he talked to me about putting schools on ocean liners to ride out storms and other natural disasters, and about putting ecosystems in floating domes. His teeth moved while he talked, but his eyes were as bright as the latest state quarters. "What do kids like?" he said. And before I could answer, he went, "Athletics! So the first thing I do is, I walk in and say, 'Quick show of hands: Who here would like to swim five miles to school?'"

"I bet they would like that a lot," I said, the house getting closer. I took one last swig of coffee, chewed on the grounds, spat them out.

"It's the hundred-mile zoo," he said.

"There would be animals?"

"Exotic animals! And in their natural habitats. Endangered ones. Kids would swim to school through the glassed-in canals and look at them."

I told him that sounded pretty fucking incredible.

"This is good. You're giving me ideas," he said, easing the throttle and making a vaguely circular gesture with his free hand.

I told him the feeling was mutual, and before we knew it, we were there. He tied up the boat and he waited for me, even though I didn't ask him to. I carefully carried the mushroom up the rocks, spilling half its dew on me. I set the pot down and tore off my shirt. Steam rose from my flesh. I balled the shirt and stuffed it in my back pocket. I picked the pot back up and headed toward the house, where I banged on the cellar door—the only way in, far as I could see. I waited. The dude in the boat squinted. He was talking to the sun. There was no answer. I banged again. I tried the knob, but it was locked. I shouted, "Rob! Rob! Rob!"

I looked up at the house's second story and set the pot down, again. I grabbed hold of a stone column and scaled it onto the front porch. I looked for an open window, but found none. I wrapped my fist in the sweatshirt, smashed the cheapest-looking window, and climbed through it. I cupped my junk and carefully hooked my leg over the jagged glass stalagmites.

The house was like something that had slowly and naturally grown atop the rock: a coral reef or a mussel cluster. Many Robs could've lived in it. A colony. I called Rob's name, and it echoed throughout the house. I opened doors and looked in, but all the rooms were empty. I looked in each one and called Rob's name. I looked out of every window. You could see out in every direction. You could see the sea or the bridge or the town, still asleep. On the top floor there was a big window over the bed, and the glass was missing—just gone. I blinked at the wind that rushed through. Down below, the guy in the boat was just sitting there, talking. The sun rose behind the clouds. "Hey," I yelled down, "can you take me back?"

"We need to find my friend's glasses," he yelled. "We've got to check the dump!"

"Okay," I yelled back. "I'll help you find them." I took one last look around, but there was nothing other than one room that looked out only onto the water and smelled like Rob when he wasn't doing well. I looked for blood or burns, but didn't see any. I stood in the middle of the house with my hands on my hips and looked around. I made a slow circle.

"My friend can't see without them!" the guy yelled.

Coffee sloshed in my guts and up near my heart. Rob would be back, I told myself. I shut my eyes, saw his thumb hooked over the rim of a diner mug and into the hot, wet black. There was nothing more I could do, and I wanted to be there for whoever needed me. I gripped the sill, brought my leg over the broken window glass. The guy's swears were getting louder. "Listen," I shouted. "I'm here to help!"

(......)

A diner-shaped hole: These absent landmarks must vex out-of-towners hoping to follow a local's directions. ("Take a left where Custy's used to be," we tell them. Or "It's just past the old milk store, on the right.") But it would be awfully small of them not to see how a memory might remain more real than whatever took its place.

. . . the new kids: Meaning the new Browns and RISDs: reinforcements for the Occupying Forces. They parade through Providence, taking whatever's left from our gutted thrift shops and Salvation Armies before moving on to Brooklyn or San Francisco so they can begin their lives for real, while the whole time we locals watch, waiting, aging. But they stay young. They get younger every year.*

I've watched this four-year cycle turn over six times now. Back when I went to college, they all wore mid-'60s Mod and Nouvelle Vague: skinny ties, anoraks, and raincoats for guys, and girls in toreador pants. By Eli's senior year they'd moved on to '70s bells and stripey hip-huggers and too-tight double knits with collars as wide as gull wings. And now they've reclaimed the mid-'80s mainstream: Members Onlys and the same high-waisted acid-wash jeans and top-of-the-food-chain iron-on sweatshirts—lions or wolves in their natural habitats—that bottom-of-the-sex-chain student security volunteers used to wear without irony in high school. I figure it can't be all that long before RISD kids start dressing in baggy jeans and triple-XL aqua tees. But sooner or later the past will catch up to all of us, and things will start going backward for real.

> *It might interest you to know that up until now, I have only once managed to bully someone other than myself. The child in question was a pampered ten-year-old Venezuelan named Shimon Vainrub. I was eighteen at the time, working as a junior counselor at the same sleep-away camp in Athol, Massachusetts, where I, too, had spent a particularly unhappy prepubescent summer.* Young Shimon was assigned to my cabin, along with all the other homesick foreigners, bed wetters, and milksops. Shimon—then heir to a vast oil fortune recently wrested from his family by Chavez—had little interest in mess hall meals as he regularly received care packages of gummy colas, chocolate stars, and gas-station arepas. So I took to quizzing him:
>
> > *Me:* What did we have for lunch, Shimon?
> > *Shimon:* Ehh . . . meat.
> > *Me:* What kind of meat?
> > *Shimon:* Ehhhhh . . . *cheese.*
>
> I would then take away his *Condorito* funny books and make him wear a box over his head and repeat "I am a

rotten person" for the remainder of postcard hour. *Mala-leche,* Shimon used to hiss at me when he thought I was asleep. *Mala-leche. Mala-leche. Mala-leche.*

I had arrived at Camp Miskatonic only to discover that the rocketry and archery for which I had signed up in advance had both been canceled. During counselor-training week, the Welsh demolitions enthusiast hired to run both courses had been fired for putting alum into the CIT coordinator's lube. I cried myself to sleep every night and woke up adhered to the plastic mattress. Having already seen more than my share of prison movies, I quickly sought the one camper even less well liked than myself, finding him in the quiet, linty person of Jeremiah Katz-Polk. While waiting behind him on chow line, I told Polk he stunk and was a jerk *and* a homo, whereupon he spun around and punched me twice in the heart. I then went seven days without showering or moving my bowels and, much to my bunkmates' delight, got sent home humiliated and doubled over with searing gas pain.

Recently reimagined as a role-playing day camp called Warriors & Wizards. Yet another example of my having come of age at the wrong time. And that goes double for Eli.

*Just when I think I'm done losing him . . . I find myself wishing the years were people so I could punch them right in their exed-out faces.

Tandem: Could this be the same two-seater Eli won, on a dare, for batter-dipping, deep-frying, and then eating his own jockey shorts? (Managed only a bite or two, but that's all it took.)

I took the long way around to avoid hills: Had Cliff been less distracted and/or in better shape, he'd've almost certainly biked west down Harris, hooking a left at Atwells, then somehow not seeing, to his immediate right, One Eagle Square, burned into a pit of bricks and ash earlier that week.*

*But we all steered clear, for one reason or another.

My friend's glasses: Eli lost his all the time. They turned up everywhere: the bank, compost heaps, parking lots in Warwick, the lenses scuffed, the temples taped. He'd find them on the street and realize how long it had been since he'd read a book, and how much books had meant to him, once. Not that any of it could sink in anymore, but still. He used to be so sharp. I hate when I forget about him—even for a minute—or when I remember how I used to forget all about him, and for long stretches of time, too. Why, I'd go weeks without giving him a second thought. We all would, I bet, whoever *we* were. At some point after he had lost his last pair, they closed the library nearest his apartment for good.

CLASS HISTORY

Jacob Deinhardt

(Senior Class President, the Amos Fox School)

Providence Congregational Church, June 17, 1989

HELLO. HERE WE ARE! WE MADE IT.

Now, we're meant to pat ourselves on the back, but if you don't mind, I'd much prefer to talk about who isn't here.

(And by that I don't mean Eli and Alix, though I mean them, also. Of course I mean them. No, I just don't mean Slepkow, who only ate some bad clams at his old man's work picnic. Get well soon, buddy!)

Mostly I mean those we're meant to forget on a day like this. So look to your left and to your right and notice who's not there. See who didn't make it, for one reason or another. Remember him? Or her? From fire drills and field trips or cheating off you in bio? This is what history feels like. It feels like missing article you swore was there until you had to read the thing in front of everyone.

Bartek Scovic was the first kid in our class to come and go, just like that.

[SNAP FINGERS INTO MIC]

Bartek pretended to be retarded and had a little sister who actually was retarded, or maybe just lead-poisoned, and a dad who didn't live with them. He sat with Slepkow and me at lunch, but we didn't like him. He had an outdoor voice both in and out of doors and probably crapped in the cloakroom and might have eaten it also, depending on who you talked to. Bartek could fit his whole fist in his mouth, and when he did, the kids who told him to would punch him till he bit down hard on his own wrist, the blood—when he drew blood—running up it.

In third grade his dad got stopped at the state line with women in his trunk. The morning after the news broke, remember how our homeroom teachers told us how we would all have to be careful not to bring it up? Bartek was gone for good, but that didn't mean we didn't learn the lesson. We can't help who our fathers are.

Betsy Buckley was the next to go. Fifth grade. But back in kindergarten—without warning, bargaining, or otherwise quid-pro-quoing—Betsy showed me hers. She did it quickly, from across the courtyard. I didn't get a good look, but that night my mother and I argued about whether or not girls had penises until she dragged out the old man's magazines from beneath their bed.

In fourth grade, on the bus back from a whale watch, Betsy put my name on a list of gross boys that was getting passed around. I crumpled the list and brought up the time in the courtyard. Betsy denied it from two rows away. I asked her why on earth I would make it up. "Because you're weird," she said more than asked. "And gross?" "At least I don't have a penis," I said. My ears were hot, like my old man's get when he's upset.

Oh, and he's not here either. Tomorrow's Father's Day. It's like a two-in-one.)

Then came Bob Sadwin, who chased me around the play structure until someone told. Bob had no idea what it was all about, and I wouldn't admit a girl who liked him and not me because, like most girls, she only liked jerks.

And Steve Taglitelle, who left his left ball on a fire hydrant he BMX'ed into the same weekend I got the worst poison ivy. It looked like a suit of swollen skin, and scratching it felt like coming in slow motion. We both had to miss the freshman retreat to New Hampshire or wherever. From our couches we watched *Family Affair* to *Brady Bunch* and called each other twice a day. "Now how am I gonna impregnate all the best-looking girls?" he asked me. "Maybe you could impregnate the less-good-looking ones," I told him, but he started crying, and I hung up—accidentally, I think; my cheek was bigger than normal. Steve wasn't nearly as conceited as most of the boys I knew at Fox.

And little Timmy DeWolf, who dressed like Tom Cruise in *Risky Business*, then Tom Cruise in *Top Gun*, and now Tom Cruise in *Cocktail* or *Rain Man*, maybe. Or maybe he's on to John Cusack in *Say Anything*.

And Skip Daly, who returned from his first and last Fox spring break with a Mohawk, a black eye, and a Polaroid of himself leaning against a Chevette with two older girls, one of whom was basically not wearing pants. The next time I saw Skip, he was wrestling the mayor's daughter outside that wizard shop where Amy Carter worked when she went to Brown. They laughed, and I crossed the street.

Next to last was Viv Goddard. You all know about the pool party. But you don't know that Slepkow only yanked it out because he thought the tampon string was a loose hem on her swimsuit—and even if it was, then what? Make a wish? Meanwhile, Viv took the opportunity to say you know what, forget this place, and no one blamed her because she was cool like a boy and smart like a girl. Slepkow stuck around for the brunt of it because why not, and like I said, he can't think ahead.

Last was Alix, but that's a lot fresher in our minds.

Me, I've been here since kindergarten. They call us survivors, like it's an ordeal, and I suppose it has been, in its way. But you should've seen the face my father made when he heard that's what we were called. It was the same face he made when he saw the swastikas in the dome of this church.

[LOOK UP, POINT, WAIT A BEAT]

Later, in an old album, I would find a photograph of his father in a Nazi uniform. "Jaki!" he yelled, his ears red. "What?" I asked, putting the album back under his bed. He said nothing, shaking. I asked what again. "I only have my German," he said, and walked out of the room.

Teachers came and went, too.

There was Jonathan, the history teacher who failed a quarter of the class and called on dumb kids for a laugh and taped snapshots of senior girls to his office door. We heard he wasn't allowed in Connecticut. One time a carful of soccer captains tried to follow him home, and he led them all the way to the Cape before ditching them in a rotary. It was a school night.

And the old middle school head, Harry, who hid whiskey in his desk drawer. "Lavoris," he'd say, winking, when anyone caught him taking a slug between classes. He had nicknames for all the boys. "Look, it's Ragged Dick," he'd say, leaning into his office door. "Here comes the Last Angry Man!" he said to more than one of us, even though we all had reason to think he meant only us. "Dill!" he said. "Quick! How many buttons on Mickey Mouse's trousers?" We cried when Ned finally talked him into retiring. What would he do? Where would he live?

And now, as you know, this is Ned's last year, also. Or was meant to be? Either way, we'll get an earful before the day's out, so I'll just say that when he first took the job, I thought he was Ronald Reagan. He had the same blue or gray suit, the same weird wet hair, the same TV smile. But Ned acted more like Nixon, and once yelled at the entire school after someone wrote NEVER FORGET on the boys' room mirror in his own shit.

(I'm looking at where you aren't, Bartek. Right between where Bob Sadwin and Pete Siemens would be sitting. Poor Pete never stood a chance.)

But before all of them, back when both my folks worked and before I took the city bus home, I stayed late with the other Quaker half-day kids. They hired a series of people to watch us. They weren't much older than babysitters, but every bit as between things. These were the sons and daughters of parents' friends, or something. They got paid like two, three bucks an hour, and some were worse than others.

I can't remember anything about the worst one except for how she looked like a foreign or silent film star, and whenever it was just her and me, I'd get a stomachache that turned into only feeling like I had to pee. And she wore a pet rat. Is that even possible? I couldn't tell anyone, because I didn't know what to say. She smelled like rum and pencils, and what I don't know feels like she crossed it out, over and over again. I hold the paper to the light, but there's only glare.

I still see her old man, who knew my old man somehow, picking fights in the Dunkin' Donuts down the street from where I live. He seems not to own a coat, and calls everyone "sonofabitch," even women. "You sonofabitch," he says, poking them in the stomach. "You're getting soft." On the way to school, I also pass his wife, smoking on her stoop and looking around like someone who doesn't want to be lookout but has no choice. She clutches her robe and ashes into where the bushes used to be.

You're already sick of how I feel about Alix, but I will say that I made an okay painting of the art room sink and gave it to her because she said she liked it and I love her. When it became clear she liked someone else—there's no point in saying who—I asked for it back because I could be a dick, too, if that's what she wanted. She looked hurt. "But I love it," she said, in tears, touching the painting. "Fine," I said, thrilled by those tears. My hurt felt like something my father couldn't digest: hot sauce, melted cheese, fried squid. On the drive home, I pulled over twice to throw up, but couldn't.

And we all know about Eli. Just like we all know about Alix and Viv.

When they, meaning the heads of school, Ned and the new one and the other one, tried to corner Eli in the hallway after the last class he would ever teach—ours: we had been discussing Leonard Michaels's "In the Fifties" for the third or fourth time that semester because we still didn't get it, and no, Eli said, he hadn't gone to school in the fifties, he hadn't even been born yet, *for Pete's sake!*

Is that how you people read stories? Like they're only about whoever writes or reads them? Like it's gossip? You're all hopeless solipsists!—he made a break for it and ran right past them, down the stairs, out the side door, and across the street. We rushed to the window and watched him disappear down Angell. "Run, Eli!" some of us yelled. I kept on watching even after everyone left. We had no idea he was so fast.

I've recycled bits and pieces of my never-collected "In the Fifties" response here. "In the Eighties," I titled it. "No, no, no," Eli had said, folding my draft into an airplane that only turned upside down and hit him in the chest. I picked it up and unfolded it. "You see!" he said, snatching it from me and shaking it like a prop. "It's still the sixties, but with coke and synthesizers where the pot and horns used to go. Plus vests." I told him I didn't get it. "Just think of what you would have told them if you could," he said, grinning, like he had planned the whole thing. Eli just about lives for callbacks and running jokes.

Meanwhile, several girls—too many to name—all in possession of clear skin, sharp minds, and slim figures, pretty much stopped eating. And an equal number of boys, despite having grown up in loving, supportive homes, grew defensive and bitter and cruel. Lousy students discovered an escape and an excuse in drugs. Shy, hopeful boys found ways to make girls laugh in beer. Homosexuals got mocked ceaselessly and without mercy and were either strengthened or weakened by the experience, depending on what kind of people they were, because everyone is different. Kids of all kinds were turned into examples, then metaphors. Some laughed, and the rest didn't. And we—meaning us—made it.

But I'm not like the other ones who've been here all along—I won't call us survivors—Sterner, Linton, Kahn, the one who won't even look at me. Whenever I lost my gloves, my mother would tell me to take some from the lost and found, and my folks only had jobs, not things they did or were, until they didn't. I was two when my family got evicted from Belair Avenue, so for as long as I can remember, I've lived on the second floor of a bathroom-green, vinyl-sided triple-decker on the wrong side of Hope. Unless I'm getting a ride from Slepkow, I tell people to drop me off at the gray Cape around the corner. I linger at the lawn's edge till they leave, then take the back door up.

When I first came to Fox, I thought I was just like everybody else. But then, during my first week in kindergarten, I got invited over a kid's house to play. The place had turrets and a garage that was an extra house. His mom sat around all day reading magazines.

In fifth grade this exact same kid used what my old man calls American logic to explain why he didn't have to give me back my Indians cap, even though he'd found it exactly where I'd lost it the week before. I said, "How do you know I don't have lice?" He threw my hat into poison ivy. Years later, when the school temporarily moved the holiday pageant from this church on account of the swastikas, he derailed Quaker Meeting by saying the whole thing was stupid and smiling as though none of it mattered, because to him it didn't. Fuck you, I thought. Fuck you. Fuck you, fuck you, fuck you.

Wait, where was I?

I know.

When my old man stopped going to work, he handed me his car keys. The car was a rusted-out Corolla four-speed with an electric hole where the cigarette lighter should've been. That fall it got stolen, and a girl I'd known since kindergarten asked me why my parents didn't just buy me a new one. I wanted to tell her why, but I didn't. I couldn't?

My pal Slepkow's had his own car since junior year, but he mostly uses it to deliver pizzas and to bring his little sister places. He's as American as a Jew can be to the son of a German, but is only afraid of girls and of throwing up. In kindergarten I'd tease him about his egg-shaped head until he'd call me ex-friend. Instead of saying sorry, I'd start in on Bartek, and that almost always did the trick.

My family never had company, except for when my mom was out of town—for work—and my old man's friends would show up, reeking, fidgeting, hardly touching their soup. "I sometimes get electric shocks in my sleep," a guy called Shithead told me before climbing into the just-pulled-out trundle. "So if I wake up screaming, don't mind me." I found these men terrifying, authentic. Same with the mustached dudes upstairs who wouldn't buy my raffle tickets and got into fistfights every other weekend, but who played the kind of records my folks hadn't since the seventies—the kind where they left in mistakes—and would ink my Green Arrow pencils whenever I asked.

My dad would call his parents when he needed to hear their German, their Berlin logic. I never met them. They died one after the other, just weeks apart. "It's not my home anymore," he told me. I asked him if here was, and he shook his head. "I am split in two." He came here in the sixties to paint and live outside history. "No one tells you you can't do anything in this country, and look what you get," he would say after some beers and after my mom had gone to bed because she had to be up early. "Toys of cartoons of toys! Movies where two policemen at first are not friends! Art only about itself! Poison ivy! You people deserve Reagan! You deserve Bruce Willis. You deserve his gas wines."

Here's how it went for my old man: first the factory he worked in burned down the night after he dreamed it would, then he stopped trying to teach me German, then he stopped speaking it, then he stopped going to work, then he stopped getting out of bed. "Don't put your finger in that hole, Jaki," he said. Then he rolled over and went back to sleep. It was springtime, and the uncurling leaves, tender and yellow, offered little shade. I closed the blinds and waited outside for Slepkow to pick me up. High school wasn't over yet, but it felt like the end of something.

I wish Slepkow was here. And Alix and Bartek and all the rest. Those who wanted to be, at least. So not Eli. Viv never wanted to be here, either, I don't think. My old man . . . Fuck this place, they all think. But here we are. And this is the last time we'll be able to use the word *we* to describe us in the present tense, and that's what matters. The past year I've spent an awful lot of time thinking about how I wasn't loved back. But right now, behind this podium, I feel loved.

And no, that last bit isn't a *Police Academy* reference. Okay, it is. You know, for Slepkow. He would have laughed, so I left it in. His laugh sounds like a cough. I'll miss him. But believe me when I tell you I will miss every single one of you in one way or another.

(......)

. . . *MY EARS WERE HOT*: I GET THIS, TOO. AND NOT JUST FROM shame—also from wine, fire.

Liked someone else: And less than a year later they were through, for good. But even so, it's hard not to think of Passover 1990 as anything other than the last time Eli, Libby, and I were all in the same room together. Eli wept during the Four Questions that he—as the youngest—still had to ask. He excused himself and lay down on the living room rug, tears in his ears. Libby went to talk to him, but the rest of us just dug in. What can I say? We were hungry, and thought it was about his job, and we'd already had an earful.

Ned: Alix's old man spent the better part of his daughter's senior year putting out fires. In addition to covering up her extracurriculars, he also was forced to write a pointed and what would end up being heavily edited letter to *Sports Illustrated*, which, in a piece on AstroTurf,* had referred to Amos Fox as a "twenty[*sic*]-year-old prep school whose very name suggests either cleverness or craziness." There was also the brand-new Headmaster's House, for which he himself—over the board's strenuous objections**—had raised the funds. "This is my up-yours," he said, stroking a stud in the nearly completed kitchen. "And now I'll live in it. By god, I'll die here."

*An alumnus who struck it rich in the Gulf had gifted the school with its very first installation a quarter century earlier, in the then newly built DeWolf Gymnasium.

**Upon learning of this latest end run, they demanded Ned's resignation, and he responded by replacing the entire board with former squash partners.

The city bus home: So didn't I. "Here you go," said Grandpa Ike, handing me a roll of tokens and a house key necklace, plus a couple bucks' worth of change and some mixed-in mints. "Now you can be like a normal kid who lives in a regular city for a change." I got looks from the public high schoolers in the back, because they knew I was a Fox student—the bus stops just past its wrought iron gates. I soon took to catching the bus home three stops earlier so people would think I went to St. Jude's. To sell it, I'd even change into a blue dickey, a white spread collar, and a clip-on in a sub shop men's room before catching the 3:10 home.*

*Eli, who went to public Hope and required no such plausible deniability, nevertheless dressed like a Levittown mortician.

My folks had jobs: Jake had attended Fox on full scholarship, thanks both to his raw foot speed and the limited earning potential of his scatterbrained mother and bedridden father. After graduating near the top of an underachieving class, Jake would go on to earn a promptly regretted city planning degree, ride out his early twenties writing grants for nonprofits, and make a killing in development or whatever. But few know that he actually made his real mint as a college sophomore by suing the pants off his future alma matter. As a resident of his school's only *fully* coed dorm, he had severed his Achilles tendon on a rusty strip of shower-stall flashing* and settled out of court for a sum large enough to enable him to purchase for his recently widowed mother a stately four-bedroom Victorian at the intersection of Benefit and Jenckes.

*A horrific injury, no doubt, but had the school's counsel known that the fault lay more with Jake's future wife than with Buildings & Grounds, the settlement would've at the very least shrunk. Here's what really happened: while showering in the stall next to his, the future Hannah Deinhardt, then a more or less perfect stranger, had bravely slipped her shapely foot beneath the divider, laid it atop Jake's, and proceeded to scrub herself to climax. The ever-opportunistic Fox alumnus, not at all sure to whom this slender, hairless extremity belonged, nevertheless availed himself of what he immediately grasped to be a once-in-a-lifetime opportunity and, bracing himself against the stall divider, jerked off onto her painted toes. Correctly judging the substance too warm and sticky to be soap, Hannah quickly withdrew her foot, causing Jake to slip in a puddle of his own ejaculate and slice open his heel on that ragged strip of razor-sharp white metal. While the bathroom filled with Jake's bloodcurdling screams, a flushed Hannah shot open her curtain, grabbed her towel, and split, leaving Jake to stanch his wound with a washcloth. From the smoking lounge, Jake's future wife called campus security to report an urgent but undisclosed situation unfolding in the second-floor bathroom. "Please hurry," she gasped. The following morning, a chastened Hannah knocked at crutches-bound Jake's door clutching a bouquet of bleeding hearts and wearing a pair of open-toed mules. Together they rode out the semester playing variations on

Nurse and Soldier (Socialite and Photojournalist being their absolute favorite).

Swastikas: Nine years and five months earlier I had for the first and last time rung bass-clef handbells at the Fox Holiday Pageant, annually held at the same Congregational church in which we traditionally commenced.* At some point during the festivities a yawning Grandpa Ike had looked up at the church's dome and noticed the right-facing swastikas encircling it. With that, he stormed out (mere minutes, mind, before my largely inaudible solo run in "Good King Wenceslas") and began drafting on his dashboard a letter of complaint to the school, the postscript of which indexed, to the nickel, just how much money he had spent on my and my sister's educations. An emergency Friday-night Quaker Meeting was called. When everybody's least favorite history teacher told Grandpa Ike that the ornament to which he objected was *not* the Nazi insignia, but in fact the ancient Sanskrit symbol for well-being later so perversely inverted by Hitler, Ike said, "Not anymore it ain't." She theatrically turned to face the person to her right, and Ike said, "Look, I fought under Patton. We freed Buchenwald.** And nowadays a swastika's a swastika."

*Our class's graduation was moved to the smaller, less pretentious Friends Hall, where it would stay until the school's bicentennial, in 1989. It's a lovely space, but far too small for extended family, so grandparents—including, briefly and ironically, Ike and Tillie—were asked to wait outdoors while, inside the humid oaken hall, girls dressed in white linen crossed and recrossed their sticky legs, thinking of cool church stone and, I don't know, snacks? Sugarless snacks? What do girls even think about? What must they get used to? Heels? Balls? The Holocaust? From the dais, I tried to catch Eli's eye, but he was every bit as distracted.

**The only time Grandpa Ike ever mentioned his service. But the war came up all the time. On weekday mornings he would take me out for eggs at a breakfast place up the street. The only other customer that early in the day was a plump gentleman of indeterminate age and ethnicity who always ate Adam & Eves on a raft with a lime rickey on the side. Ike bought me two scrambled with toast and OJ. I always envied the fat man's breakfast and eventually worked up the nerve to say as much to Ike. "You can't drink soda first thing, and wet yolks make you sick," he said. "How come he can, then?" I asked, nodding at our fellow regular. I've never seen Ike so angry. "How can you even ask that after what he's been through?" he said, pointing with his butter knife at the blue, scratched-at tattoo on the man's flounder white forearm. I now know that the man couldn't have been more than a child at the time. "For Christ's sake, kid. Smarten up."

". . . I wake up screaming . . .": Me, I sleepwalk. It started shortly after Eli was moved from his crib first to the bottom, then the top bunk in what was now our room. Worst was when I turned eight and tumbled down two whole flights of stairs. Pa rushed up from his basement workshop and held me in his arms, kissing my bruises. It was the fastest he ever moved. His arms were warm, and I went limp in them. He smelled like his pipe. It felt like being born.

Jubilee

Mark Slepkow

KATHY SAID WE SHOULD USE OUR MILES DOWN TO D.C. AND SURprise Jake for his thirty-first, but I told her I didn't want to see their baby. Kathy said I was being dumb: we weren't there to help. Besides, Jake's kid was healthy, and that's what mattered, so I shouldn't be afraid. First I told her I wasn't afraid. Then I said, "Okay, but we won't bring Bob."

"Why?" Kathy said.

"Because," I told her, "it'll only make Jake feel bad."

Kathy said I could be like a brick sometimes. "They want to see our son too, Mark. It's not a contest."

I tried again. "Look, we'll all go, so long as I don't have to see them change it. That's where I draw the line."

"Him." Kathy sighed. "Change *him*."

"Either way," I said. "No changing."

Jake's kid was born a couple weeks after ours and came out wrong—half boy, half girl. I guess technically he's a boy, but still. His stuff's all up inside him, like a girl's. This is the kind of thing that happens on a talk show or maybe on the news when it turns into a lawsuit or an issue, but not to someone you know.

Jake is my best friend, even though I'm not sure what grown-ups mean by that—like we still need best friends, or can even keep them, what with work and wives and kids and whatnot. I didn't think I needed any friends anymore, but Jake was having a hard time, and all of a sudden I wanted to help. I figured we could leave the kids with the girls, catch a game, grab some beers—regular guy stuff like that. Plus, I don't think Kathy and I were giving each other everything we needed at this point. I wasn't holding up my end, at least, and I don't just mean in bed. Everyone always adds "in bed" to the end of everything, like you're a fortune-cookie fortune. No. I only mean we didn't talk about our days much, only Bob's, and once he went down, we were too beat for anything other than some takeout or microwave we'd eat too fast and a little cable Kathy'd fall asleep in front of. Even when we agreed, we were arguing. At one point it got so bad that I asked Kathy why she married me. "Because," she said, pausing long enough for me to think that was her answer, "I knew you could never ever hurt me."

Kathy's father died in a car before she was even born. Boyfriends came and went. "You're a good man," she added. I should've asked her what she meant. If I asked her now, I'd probably get a different answer, and I want to know what she meant at that exact moment, with both of us yelling and crying and getting ready for bed.

Jake's wife, Hannah, was in on the surprise. She picked us up at the airport with Alex in tow. It was early Friday afternoon, and Jake was still at work. Kathy sat in back between the babies, and I rode shotgun. Bob's ears never popped on the plane, but now, down on the ground, he finally slept. Meanwhile, Alex spilled out of his car seat, awake and staring. Jake had told me over the phone that the testosterone shots made Alex bigger than normal, made his bones thicker, but I was shocked all the same. He could've eaten Bob for lunch, and my son was a good two months older. I looked at Alex and caught myself thinking about locker rooms and urinals and the backseats of cars. I turned around and faced the road, but I couldn't help but check the rearview every couple seconds.

Alex looked like a normal baby boy, and I guess that's what spooked me most. Human babies are pretty weird animals, at least compared to, like, a baby fox or a snake. We're all soft and dumb and out of proportion. Alex kept smiling those weird human-baby smiles back at me, where you can't tell if it's real or if it's just gas. Those gas smiles give me the warrens. Alex wore a T-shirt with a cartoon sea horse on it. Sea horses give me the warrens, too.

"Alex seems happy," Kathy said, tugging on one of his thick, bare feet. Bob always wears socks, even in summer. Kathy thinks colds are literal, and I've given up arguing with her.

"I think he is," Hannah said, checking over her shoulder. She looked tired. Who doesn't? But Hannah looked like she had spent the night defrosting in the sink. The only other time I had ever seen her was at their wedding, which had been an open-bar blur. She had seemed hot, but not too hot. You know, relatably hot. Like a sideline reporter or lady rookie in a low-budget cop flick. A local weather girl. That's Jake's type: the kind of girl that guys who are basically realistic fantasize about. I wish I had a type.

Hannah was still hot, but less hot. Maybe teacher hot. And extra tired. As for the wedding, I only really remembered meeting her brother. He had a fucked-up arm he hid inside the sleeve of his coat. It looked like a chicken wing or maybe one of those dinosaur arms: you know, the little girly ones that the real big kind have. I actually didn't see the little arm until later, so at first I thought he only just had the one good one, like maybe he had lost the other somehow.

"We don't have these in Rhode Island," I said, interrupting the girls, who were talking about something.

"Don't have what?" Hannah said, switching lanes.

"These roads that look like normal roads, but you can drive like it's the highway."

We came to a stoplight.

"And with stoplights," I added. Hannah kind of nodded, and they went back to talking about the babies or whatever. Whatever. At least I didn't interrupt them to point out a taco joint you could tell used to be an IHOP, like I had thought to.

Hannah and Jake's development was called Jubilee, which is exactly the kind of thing I would've never stopped busting Jake's balls about back in the day. "Jubilee!" I said, laughing.

"Yeah, Jake still won't call it that."

"There used to be all kinds of things he wouldn't call what was on the menu," I said. "Going to Friendly's with him was a real pain in the ass."

The guard lifted the arm and waved us in.

"We know it's not much to look at," Hannah said as we pulled up to their place, "but we didn't have much choice in this school district, and Jake and I think History class is more important than history." You could tell this was something she had said before. It sounded like Jake.

Thirty years ago Jake's house would've been like his neighbors' house and like their neighbors' neighbors'. Now they know to offer different kinds of driveway shapes and shutter colors and crap like that. But these shutters were all screwed on. Even if you could shut them, they still wouldn't be big enough to cover the glass.

Hannah gave us the grand tour. The front door was heavy but delaminating. Huh, I said to myself while the girls got the boys settled. Last we talked, Jake told me the house was sinking—he had put jacks in the basement to hold up the low spots. Which was one thing, but Jake made a lot of money at his job in planning or PR or whatever. I never did get around to asking him what he meant when he said PR, if that's even what he said. Now it was too late. He'd think I was a real asshole if I asked him what he did for a living all of a sudden. I've got to start paying attention the first time around. But whatever he does at work, I bet the only boxes they talk about are the kind they need to think outside of.

They had lots of furniture, that's for sure. In what Hannah called his den, Jake had an executive-style desk and one of those programmable chairs to go along. While the girls talked blinds, I fooled around with it for a while, but I'm no good with stuff you adjust. I do know from different kinds of actual boxes, though. I could tell you all about J-17's and J-20's, but I try to leave the job at home. Kathy's had her fill. Besides, she's the real breadwinner, so if anything, we talk about her work. But I don't mind. Sometimes, in the shower, I daydream about all these men flirting with her to get jobs. In my daydreams Kathy's a lot meaner than in real life. She lines them all up in her office and calls them ladies and steps on their penises. Sometimes it even works, until I remember that Kathy says she'd never, ever have an affair, but if she did, it would probably be with a woman. That's not a turn-on for me. I feel useless enough as it is.

When I was through with the chair, I joined the girls in the living room. The kids were lying on the floor in front of the couch. Bob reached over and grabbed a fistful of Alex's cheek. Alex shook his head and swatted him away. He was more into the wooden blocks Hannah had scattered between them than my son was, which is also normal. He had long, thick eyelashes, though, which I used to think were a sign of male gayness.

"The place looks great, Hannah," Kathy said.

"We tried," she said. "Can I get you guys anything to drink? Some juice or soda?"

"I'd love a Diet Coke," Kathy said.

"How about you, Mark. Can I get you something?"

"Got any beer?"

Kathy looked at me. She didn't like when I drank without her. She was always afraid I'd get carried away. These days I'm much more likely to get carried away with food than with beer, but she looked at me just the same.

"We don't usually keep beer," Hannah said. "Jake's more of a wine guy these days. But I think we might have some left from the Oscars. In the mini-fridge in the garage. Let me check."

"Don't worry about it. I can always take soda."

"Oh, no bother. Just let me check." Hannah walked out of the living room.

"Why couldn't you just have a soda?" Kathy said.

"I don't know, beer might be nice."

"But she didn't offer you a beer. She said juice or soda."

I thought about it some more. "We're on vacation."

"You shouldn't make her go through any extra trouble. Things are hard enough. And it's not vacation, it's just a trip."

I looked down at Bob. He was touching Alex's face again. Alex blinked, turning away from our son and toward the doorway.

Hannah came back into the living room carrying two glasses of soda and a bottle of beer. "We only had light beer," she said, passing me the bottle. "I hope that's okay.

"Gotta keep an eye on my girlish figure," I said, patting my gut. Kathy shot me a look. I didn't get why at first, but then, after a second, I thought, shit. Maybe Hannah hadn't heard me. I tend to say the kinds of things people don't really hear. I took a sip. It was that bitter, foreign kind, but it tasted good, watery and cold.

It was true, though, that I'd put on weight since the baby. I had always thought it was the woman who got fat. Except for first thing in the morning, I can barely see helmet when I'm taking a leak. I hardly know how to dress away from work. I can never decide whether to tuck in or not. These days, I change in the dark.

We all drank our drinks and watched Alex play with blocks. He was really concentrating on stacking them straight. Where his eyebrows would've been if he had any was all red, and his mouth was just an *O*.

"Alex is so smart, you can tell," Kathy said. "Look at him handle those blocks! He's a little architect."

"He loves to stack things," Hannah said.

"That's amazing for a kid his age. It really is," Kathy said. Bob looked at us and grinned bubblegum gums and a couple choppers. Then he rolled onto his back and looked at us upside down, laughing. I smiled back at my son and half-ass peekabooed from behind my beer. It's funny, some days Bob'll look like me, and other days he looks just like Kathy, like there's this tug-of-war inside him. I once heard that all kids start out like their dad so he won't eat them.

I hope Kathy's genes win, and so does she, I bet. Kathy even wanted to name Bob Freddie, after her brother. I told her Freddie was a girl's name. I wanted to call him Stan, which was a man's name, through and through. A girl can't ever call herself Stan. But Kathy said it made her think of some old creep with green toenails eating supper in his shorts. We settled on Bob, her father's name. A kid named Bob Sadwin beat me up once in sixth grade. Chased me up the slide and just started whaling on me for putting a pen down his girlfriend's buttcrack in Math. Who's got a girlfriend in sixth grade, is what I'd like to know. Maybe my son'll be tough, too. Maybe he'll also get a girl of his own before he knows what to do with her, which is the only real way to learn how to know what to do with one when you finally get one for real. Kathy was my first, and I'm still a disappointment. "Don't rush the first time," my mom had told me, giving me the only advice she ever gave me not about school or work or being sick. My folks didn't really have any friends. Just family.

Bob picked up a block and threw it at Alex's latest work, knocking it over. I tried not to laugh. Kathy sighed. "All Bob ever does is destroy things."

"He's actually kind of a dick," I said.

"Well, he's a boy," Hannah said. After that, no one said anything for a while. I'm not sure for how long no one talked, but I do know that at some point the freezer made ice. Alex had finally given up on trying to build his tower and was now picking loose hairs out of the carpet with both hands and studying them. Bob picked up one of the knocked-over blocks and tapped Alex's back with it. Alex didn't turn around, so Bob sat down and started sucking on the corner of a blue *Q*.

Jake was a dick when we met. In kindergarten, he would sing this stupid song at me from that ad for eggs: "The Incredible, Edible Egg!" And at some point we were friends because kids will become friends or enemies for next to nothing.

But why do they even make ads for eggs? And not some eggs, all eggs. I think that's wrong, ads for all of something, like all nuts or milk or diamonds. Maybe a big bright billboard for flowers on the way to work: *When's the last time you bought your wife Flowers™* or *gave her Gems™?* No one makes eggs, and you either buy them or you don't. I sell folks SlepCo boxes, not on the idea of boxes. There's no Box Council. You should put your stuff in one of our boxes, I say, not, *You Should Put Stuff in a Box!* In Rhode Island they either buy ours or Kilmartin's or none at all—not that that's an option: everything you can think of goes in a box at some point.

When Jake got home, it was like Dick Van Dyke tripping over the ottoman in the opening credits of his show, except we weren't the people he saw every day at work. I can still tell what season of a show it is just by the wife's hairstyle. It might be my only skill, apart from always knowing what time it is inside of five minutes. There's no point in saying Laura Petrie is my type. "You guys," Jake said, setting his bag-looking briefcase down on the floor. It was soft and had way too many straps, but growing up, his folks made him wear lederhosen. "Slepkow!"

"Happy birthday . . ." Kathy and I sort of sang, more or less together. Kathy got up and gave him a hug and a kiss on the cheek. Then Jake folded his jacket over the back of a chair and walked over to me. I shook his hand, and he gave me a bear hug. I could feel

Jake's hands sink into the extra flesh beneath my shoulder blades. I broke the hug, which felt weird, but only because of how fat I am now. I'm sure he could feel how fat I felt.

"Good to see you," he said, his eyes a little red, but maybe from rush hour and not feelings?

"Likewise," I said.

"And Bob." Jake squatted down to touch his head. "Look at him! Look at this little guy."

"Doesn't he look like a Stan?" I said.

"He looks just like you, Kathy," Jake said, gently running his hand over the soft spot in my son's skull. The static made Bob's thin brown hair stand on end.

"Alex is something else," I said.

I didn't even have to turn my head to know exactly what kind of look Kathy was giving me.

"He's our boy," Jake said.

We all sat down.

"So," he said, "what do you guys have planned?"

"Whatever you two want," Kathy said. "This is your guys' weekend."

"Hey, Jake," I said. "I got us tickets to the O's game tomorrow."

"Oh," said Hannah, getting up and refolding Jake's jacket the exact same way. "I hope the game is even still on."

"Why wouldn't it be?" I asked.

"A train derailed outside Camden Yards, and one of the cars was carrying toxic chemicals. They had to cancel the game tonight. It's still burning, and there's fumes."

"That's right," said Jake. "I forgot about that."

"Huh." I took a pull off my empty beer.

"Well, we'll just have to listen to the news—see what's going on," said Hannah.

"Yeah," said Jake, remembering something to his left. "There are no metaphors."

I didn't know what he meant. So I said, "But this is real," just to keep the conversation going.

Jake thought about it for a while—like three, four seconds—which I thought was generous of him. "Yes," he said finally.

"You gotta figure it'll burn off soon," said Kathy.

"Yeah, I hope so," said Jake. "That beer looks good. I think I'll go get myself one."

"Grab me another while you're at it," I said, setting my empty down on the coffee table. Kathy shot me another look. She was also slapping one shoe up and down on her foot and bouncing her leg—I could feel the flesh and muscle vibrations coming through the couch cushions. It was kind of open, her shoe, so you could see her whole foot almost—like a goddess sandal. Then it struck me how brown and smooth it looked, like a caramel. Her foot is basically nude, I thought. Someone could just reach out and touch it. Does anyone ever touch the nearly nude foot of a lady while making a point? Is that how you let her know that you do want to fuck? By lightly touching her foot while looking her in her eyes and saying something strong and kind? I grew up in a house where no one really touched, so I don't know how these things work.

Kathy had been spending a lot of time outdoors lately, with Bob. Strolling and running behind his stroller, pushing him down the street like a snowplow or that iron skirt-looking thing on the front of an old-timey train. I really wish she wouldn't run against traffic. Lately I hadn't been looking at Kathy all that much. I could barely even recognize her. I watched her leg bounce up and down and realized I was getting hard, so I tugged at my shirttails and crossed my legs. Her real-life anger didn't usually make me feel sexual. That light beer had gone to my head like medicine. I felt like a boy again. And she just looked like some pissed-off girl, and not my wife. It was the most specific desire I'd had for her in almost two years. Plus, there was all that movement and friction.

Just as he was about to leave the room, Jake turned around. "Anyone else need anything?" he asked.

"I'm fine," Kathy said, still bouncing that leg.

"We're all set," said Hannah.

"Hey," I said to Kathy.

"How do you like your Diaper Genie?" she asked Hannah.

I reached out and touched Kathy's foot, and she crossed her legs the other way, just out of my reach. *My timing sucks,* I almost said aloud. Sometimes I'll blurt out the answer to a question Kathy asked me months ago, like she just asked it or, even worse, to one she never even thought to ask.

After dinner, the girls put the boys down: Alex in Jake and Hannah's bed, still, and Bob in what would someday be Alex's crib. Jake and I smoked cigars on the patio. They were good—not Cuban good, but close. I had picked them up in Tampa right before Bob was born and had been saving them for a special occasion. Jake and I used to smoke Swisher Sweets back in high school, so it felt good and familiar to be sitting there blowing smoke rings into the night.

"So, Jake," I said about a minute or two after I became aware of the silence.

"Yeah?" Jake asked through the cigar in his jaw.

"Nothing, I guess. Happy birthday?"

Jake laughed. "Good old Slepkow," he said. "You'll never change."

"Yeah," I said, trying to make my laughter sound like Jake's.

"I'm glad you're here, Mark."

"Me too."

"It's hard not to worry. About the future at least. Most things are only going to get worse."

"I thought this kind of thing was supposed to make you realize how lucky you are."

"Not when you stop and think about how other people really are. This is about things I can't control. I've got to be clear-eyed."

"I can see that." I didn't know what else to say, but figured it was the kind of time where I should say something helpful. Supportive. "Babies are basically wild animals," I said. "But helpless. Bob doesn't even look up when you say his name."

"Truth is, I'm angry all the time. I'm always a bad choice away from losing it entirely."

I wasn't sure whose choices he meant—his or someone else's—so I just listened. Maybe listening could help.

"Last week I was out front with Alex," he said, "and some douche in a BMW tears past us at, like, forty at least. Inside the community. So I jumped in my car and sped after him like a cop. Left Alex alone on the lawn. He could have crawled right into the street." His voice cracked a little. Just a hair. It might've even been the cigar. No more beer, and it was still hot. "Hannah was out shopping."

"Did you catch him?"

"No."

"Too bad."

"I yelled stuff out my window, but I'm not sure he heard me. He was on the phone. I just want a little justice, you know? It doesn't even matter how small. A minor victory, even. It would be like food or water to me at this point."

"Me, I get angry in the park, mostly. And sometimes just before bed."

Jake pulled a dead dandelion from a crack in the bricks and threw it into the bushes. "You're a lucky guy, Slepkow."

He said it like he was mad at me. "What do you mean?" I said.

"You've always been comfortable not knowing stuff. Me, I've got to know every last thing. I'm almost never surprised."

"Come on," I said.

"This is the first time I've been surprised since college."

"Coming down was Kathy's idea," I said a little too quickly.

"Not about that, you idiot. About Alex."

"Oh. Yeah. Of course."

We finished our cigars without talking.

The guest bed was soft and queen-size. At home we had a firm king. The air-conditioning was on full blast, so we even needed a blanket. It was central air, and we couldn't turn it down. Under the covers, Kathy's legs felt smooth and strong. Her back was to me, but we were right up against each other for a change. Normally, she didn't like to touch when we slept, but like I said, the bed was small and we were cold. I rolled onto my back. I took my penis out of my boxers and held it in my fist.

"How was your run?" I asked. She had taken a quick one after putting Bob down. She seized every chance.

"It was all right. I only did three miles. I'm falling way behind on my Ironman schedule."

"Oh." I had a hard time talking about exercise with Kathy. I could feel her impatience in her shoulder blades, which felt like scissors. She was wearing her sleeping tank top, which had nursing stains the size and shape of large, weird-shaped areolas, but it didn't mean she didn't want to have sex. For her, sex is no big deal—like exercise, she says. "It makes me feel better about myself," she says, "but it also needs to fit into my schedule. And I've already signed up for a lifetime membership."

I tried to think about how her foot had looked before, in front of everyone, but couldn't focus. I sniffed my fingers. Cigars.

"I stink," I said.

Kathy laughed. "You smell like an old man."

I held my penis some more, but it wasn't getting any harder. "I should probably shower," I said, tugging quietly.

"I got lost coming back here," she said. "All the streets look the same."

Just then the A/C clicked off, and right away the room felt like a crawl space. I could hear news coming through the wall, from

Jake and Hannah's bedroom. They had it on soft, but the walls were thin. Jake coughed once. A short, dry cough, like he was forcing it. I wondered if they would hear us. But Kathy never really got all that loud, so I tightened my grip and thought about her getting lost and winding up in someone else's house. What if nobody minded and things just went from there? A real free-for-all. A jubilee! Of course, she would have to shower first and borrow some clothes. The wife would have to be the same size. I could imagine it if I focused but also kept things a little blurry, like with *Magic Eye*. I've never been what you would call creative, and sometimes I worry that TV killed what little imagination I might've had. But with some effort I could see her and someone else's wife, who was cute enough, on a couch taking turns with a basically realistic cock attached to a guy with no face and definitely no asshole. He was nobody's husband. He was just some guy, and nobody asked any questions. They just made the most of it. They were all happy and just the right amount embarrassed. And finally I was about to roll over and follow through when I realized that my left arm had fallen asleep. I dragged it out from under the pillow, and it fell over the side of the bed like dead meat. I started rubbing it to try to wake it up, and right away I lost my sexy thoughts and my hard-on because I can only do one thing at a time. Kathy, her back still to me, went back to being my wife, who hadn't been fucked by me or anyone else in, what, ten months? People say she's out of your league like it's a good thing.

But I'm trying to be a good husband and father. I really am. A few months after Bob was born, we talked about the husband part. I said I wasn't ready yet, and she sighed. "That's okay. But still. I'm right here."

"I waited twenty-three years, what's a couple few months," I told her, like it was a joke. But she didn't take it like one. I said I was tired all the time and needed to be a good father more than a good husband right now.

"Why can't you be both?"

"I can try," I said. "But father's more important."

"They're both important," she said. "I'm right here now, Mark. But I might not always be, okay? Do you understand?"

After Kathy's father died, even with the settlement, her mother had a tough time of it, and so did Kathy and Kathy's brother. They moved around a bunch: Oxnard, Tacoma, Mobile. And Foster was worst of all. But they had family there, and that's what mattered at that point. Plus it was cheap. Her mom's car, when she even had one, was always a mess, and that drove Kathy nuts. Gum in the ashtray, nuts on the floor, maps everywhere. The way Kathy keeps her car, if there were nuts on the floor, you could eat them, no problem. At home, you could serve soup from our toilets. "We're keeping things straight and clean for Bob," she only had to say once. We split the work. She handles the bedrooms, I get the kitchen and the living room, and we alternate bathrooms. She cooks all the meals, though, because my tongue is pretty much always burned. But I set the table and clean up after and load and unload the dishwasher correctly. I also put things back where I found them and always pick things up off the floor. Our house is so well kept that even a guest would know where the stamps are. Not that we have guests, but still. We make a good team.

Around three o'clock or so, I gave up. Kathy wasn't exactly snoring, but she wasn't not snoring either. Plus, past a certain point you're better off up and about, doing things instead of lying down trying not to think about stuff. I don't ever have too much on my mind, but it can keep me up all the same, and that night, for some reason—maybe seeing Jake, maybe not being able to fuck my wife again—I got stuck thinking about a bunch of things I wish I hadn't done or said or thought. Sometimes I'll just lie there and watch it, like a terrible movie that's always on.

So I got out of bed and balls-of-the-feet sneaked downstairs to Jake's den to watch some cable. I flipped through the channels, but there was nothing good on—fishing, shopping, movies that were almost over—and that's when I saw all the DVDs piled up underneath the TV. Kid's stuff mostly, same as us, all the Baby Elmos and Beethovens and Einsteins. Then I thought to look for some porn, but no dice. Jake must've stashed it someplace special. No NC-17s either, not even the unrated European kind. So I skimmed through the R's and even the PG-13s, reading the rating criteria—Language, Intense Situations, Child Endangerment, a Sexual Conversation, a Scene of Peril, and all kinds of Violence: Medieval, Science Fiction, Fantasy, Domestic, and even Zombie, but none of the good Rs: no Sexual Situations, a Sex Scene, Nudity, Scenes of Graphic Nudity, Full-Frontal Nudity. No Brief Nudity, even. But who am I to judge? At our house, we only have the kind of movies with more than one ending, where you can't even remember if you've seen it or not. But that doesn't mean I still don't hate when Kathy falls asleep first.

I was just about to give up and watch *Rear Window*—Jews love Grace Kelly like we love golf and hotels—when I noticed a plain red envelope peeking out of the rubber-banded flat-screen manual. I opened it up and saw that it was labeled wedding video: unedited. I hit mute, slipped the disc in, and fast-forwarded through the ceremony to all the drinking and dancing and hanging out.

"Oh," I heard a little bit later. I looked up to see Hannah in an open, then closed robe, sleep-haired and slitty-eyed.

"Yes," I said, hitting pause and yanking up my boxers. The elastic waistband snap made us both wince. My fist was full of t.p.

"I heard noise," she said, and looked at the TV screen—which was paused on a shot of Kathy in this great dress I only half remembered, and that she looked like a stranger in—then away, then back at me, then at the floor.

"Can't sleep," I said.

"It's hard sometimes."

"Sorry."

"That's okay, Mark."

"I—"

"Mark . . ."

"—it's *my* wife."

"And this is *Jake's* den."

"Yes." I hit stop, and that blue DVD logo came up.

"There's a guest bathroom."

"I know."

"Back to sleep."

"Me also."

"Close up, okay?"

"Sorry."

"Good night, Mark."

"Please don't tell."

"Mark, good night."

"Please?"

The fire went mostly out at some point overnight, even though it was still smoldering a bit. But the news said that all the bad poison had burned off and the air was safe to breathe again. The girls went shopping with Alex and Bob, and Jake and I drove into Baltimore. It was a one o'clock game, so we figured we'd grab an early dinner down by the wharf afterward. Maybe get some of those crabs you crack open with hammers. I've seen those on TV.

The Angels won 6–3, but the only really interesting things that happened had nothing to do with the game. First of all, some fatso in the bleachers gave the Angels' right fielder—Tim Salmon, who's a real juicer, you can tell—a hard time all afternoon, calling him a jerk and an asshole and a cocksucker. By the bottom of the fifth he had run out of things to shout, so he goes, "Hey Salmon! Nice cocksucking cap, you cocksucker!" And, in between pitches,

Salmon turns around and says, "What! My cap?" and points to it like, what the fuck are you even talking about. I liked that. It seemed human.

The other interesting thing was at the top of the sixth inning, when a huge plume of thick black smoke floated past the park. It must have come from the tunnel where that train derailed—a big black jellyfish of a cloud with a tail like a jellyfish might have if it were a monster in D&D and made out of evil smoke instead of whatever jellies are made of. Other jellies? We both saw it in the sky at the same time.

"Oh, man," I said, pointing. "I hope it doesn't come down here."

"Christ."

But it just kept slowly floating by until it was out of sight, like a balloon some kid had let go of, back before people worried about owls and large fish dying.

There was a lot of traffic leaving the stadium. We sat there on the highway with the windows up and the A/C cranking, moving ahead a car length or two every other song. To our left was a white stretch limo. Someone had painted MICKIE'S BACHELORETTE PARTY! on the side in what looked like lipstick.

"Get a load of that," Jake said.

"I thought they just had showers."

"Not anymore. Now they all go wild. Get drunk, hire strippers. Eat penis cake."

"That's crazy," I said.

Pretty soon the limo's back windows rolled down and a sloppy-eyed woman wearing a lei poked her head out. She was screaming and waving a bottle of that stuff that tastes like lemonade but messes you up real quick. The car in front of us started honking. It was filled with big-backed college dudes in baseball hats. They rolled down their windows and leaned outside.

"Whassup," the driver yelled, like the guys in the beer commercial.

"Whassup," the woman yelled back, and disappeared into the limo. About a second later, though, her ass was sticking out the open window. Then she hiked up her skirt and gave us all an eyeful. She was wearing one of those thongs, so it was her whole ass pretty much. The guys started cheering.

"Wow," I said. "I've never seen anything like that."

"That's an ass, Mark. They're for pooping and sometimes even sex."

"Everybody's been making fun of me my whole life. But now I thought at least you'd knock it off, with what you got dealt."

Jake gripped the steering wheel tighter. He had put one of those braided leather covers on it, and it crackled in his fists. We inched up a few more car lengths, keeping pace with the limo. Then three more windows opened and three more bare asses appeared, all in a row. The guys were going nuts, screaming and clapping and honking their horn. They leaned out of their car and started chanting, "SHOW YOUR TITS!" like it was spring break or Mardi Gras or something. Then the first woman—the one with the lei—popped out of the moonroof. She waved her arms and blew the guys in the car ahead of us a great big kiss. They started chanting even louder, and the woman winked and swayed back and forth. Then she pulled up her tank top and flashed her tits. They were tan, except for where the cups of her top would have been if she'd had one on, which reminded me of the '80s. Then she disappeared back into the limo. The driver of the car leaned hard on the horn, a long, moaning honk that the guys moaned along to.

"Whoa," I said, and my face got hot and tight, and I remembered how in fourth grade I actually passed out once after the school nurse showed us a sex-ed video—it was the period part that did it. Kids drew bloodstains on my lunch sack with red markers, and we never even finished up the unit.

The limo snuck onto an off-ramp and disappeared. "Something to tell the grandkids about, huh?" I said.

Jake pulled the emergency brake back a couple clicks, then released it. He looked down and shook his head. But more to clear it than to scold me, I think. I didn't take it personal. In the rearview, the traffic rippled in the smog, like a sitcom about to flashback. Sorry sometimes makes things worse. I hadn't meant anything. It was just something to say, a figure of speech. Christ. Fully half of what I say means nothing.

We couldn't find a parking spot anywhere near the restaurant, and it was a long walk back to the car after dinner. The neighborhood was one of those no-man's-lands you find between the bars and downtown. You know: a couple auto body shops, a strip club, maybe a storage place or two. At one point a white car pulled up alongside us, slowed down. Someone inside made wet noises. Then it drove off. For a minute I thought it was the same car as the one on the highway, but then I remembered that that car had been somewhere between blue and gray.

My jeans chafed my thighs, and my shorts rode right up into the crack of my ass, parting and crushing my balls. I had to start losing weight. I felt like one of those fat river animals that get chewed up by powerboats. Manatees. Now I know the name because I looked it up on the Web when I got home, but I hadn't known it then. Supposedly sailors used to mistake them for mermaids. Granted, I've never been at sea, but if you ask me, that's one sorry-looking mermaid.

We were rounding the corner onto the street where Jake had parked when that same white car came up behind us again. Another young guy with a crew cut leaned out the window and yelled, "Faggots!" I could hear him laughing, and then I saw a flash of green. Felt a quick, sharp smack to the side of my head. Heard glass shatter against pavement. Went down on one knee, clutched my skull.

"Are you all right?" Jake asked, more than once, I'm guessing, because he yelled it more than asked it.

"Yeah, yeah, no, I'm okay. I'm okay." My head was ringing, and my eyes stung from what I quickly realized was too dark and too thick to be beer. In the streetlight the blood on my hands looked as brown as mud.

"Fuckers!" Jake yelled. "You fuckers!"

I held on to the curb and brushed glass shards from my hair. Jake grabbed the broken bottle or a different bottle and hucked it at them. It hit their rear windshield with a small, glassy burst. The car squealed to a stop and turned around. I squinted away blood and headlights and looked up to see Jake standing in the middle of the road. He burned around the edges in the bright white headlight. He screamed into the light. My knees kept folding under me. Jake ran toward the car, head up, arms pumping, as fast as ever. The car screeched to a stop. Jake banged on the hood and waved his hands like a homeless. It looked like a channel that only kind of came in, like scrambled porn. Guys piled out of the car, at least three of them. I shook my head and pushed myself up. I ran fatly over to Jake, hearing only my soles slapping concrete, and saw him go down. They were massed around him, hitting him in the face, on top of the head, kicking him in the sides and chest and ass, crushing his face with their fists. I didn't know what I would do when I got there. I tried to get there. I heard a scream I felt in my nuts. We all stopped, like it was instinct. The circle of guys pulled back and came apart, two or three of them staring at their one screaming friend, who stumbled backward holding his right hand in his left. I looked at Jake, on his knees, who spat something onto the pavement, then reached down, picked it up, and chucked it the length of the block at least. I lost whatever it was in the darkness. "Get it!" someone cried. Before I could figure out what had happened, they were running after it, then grabbing it and jumping back into their car and speeding away. I looked down at Jake, who wiped blood from his face and said, "I bit off his finger."

"Oh," I said. Jake vomited beer and crab and maybe blood onto the street. I put my hand on the top of his head to comfort him, but I didn't know what to do with it once I put it there, so I just held on to a hunk of his hair for a while and moaned. I had no idea how to make a man feel better. Jake's hair is thick like a dog's, the lucky stiff. I shut my eyes and saw jellyfish made of light. A man-of-war stung me on the arm when I was six. I blacked out on the beach and was sorry the purple scar faded because it looked tough and I wanted something to show for my troubles other than a story from my vacation that no one would believe. It's funny the things you remember, and when you remember them, and how little they have to do with anything.

Back at Jake's, the girls were watching the wedding video. We came in quietly and stood behind them, behind the couch. If they'd turned around when they said hi, they'd have seen Jake, his face swollen, his eyes wet, his broken teeth stained with blood, and his mouth crusted with puke. My head throbbed, and light hurt it. But we just stood silently and watched them watch the video. They were at the part where everyone was dancing. Except for me. I was just sitting and drinking, watching other people have fun. You could make out the back of my head just above the time stamp. From that angle I looked less bald than I felt, but every bit as fat. Then the camera zoomed in on Hannah's brother. His jacket was off now, and you could see his little arm real clearly. He held it up with his good arm when he danced, tucking its three or four fingers under his chin so it wouldn't flop around. He was pretty comfortable. Shit, why wouldn't he be? He'd already had a lot of time to get used to things. I didn't remember him dancing, though. I must've been pretty far gone at that point. The camera followed this brand-new brother to my oldest friend as he moved around the floor in great sweeping circles, dancing with all the ladies, one after another: his sister, the maid of honor, his mother, and, eventually, my wife. Kathy's dress was black velvet with these knotted portholes where you could see her squeezed-together breasts. In the shiny velvet you could see the faint outline of her belly just beginning to swell. They danced together for a while, my unborn son no bigger than a baby chick inside her. They made tear-shaped loops across the parquet, and he spun her this way and that with his one good arm. I narrowed my eyes to focus. To try to stop the pounding. I watched the tiny tips of his shiny shoes catch the light, and hold the light, and let go of the light, and slide back and forth and back again.

I just want my son to do all right in this world, better than I have at least. As for Jake's kid, I keep my fingers crossed.

Kathy's obstetrician was also a mohel—"I like to cover all the bases," he had joked, but in a way that relaxed us—and he brought his own twelve-year-old son to the hospital with him when he came to cut Bob. They were both dressed in scouts' uniforms, with badges and neckerchiefs and whatnot, because afterward they were on their way to a nature hike. I didn't even know Jews could become scouts. The doctor's son stood to his father's right and watched him as he strapped my son to the restraint chair. The boy didn't say much, but he looked at his father in a way that I don't recall ever looking at my old man—at least not past eight—and like how I would want my son to someday look at me. He wasn't smiling or frowning, just calmly paying attention.

The procedure was over pretty quick. After, the doctor handed me a brown childproof bottle with my son's foreskin in it. He told me it was a Jewish tradition for the father to dig a hole in his backyard and bury it. I thanked him and put the bottle in the breast pocket of my coat. When I got home, I put the bottle inside one of those little flowered gift boxes that Kathy likes me to bring home from time to time, and I stuck it on top of the mantel and more or less forgot about it.

You know, I'd be lying if I said that any of this meant all that much to me at the time—Dr. Gottesman and his boy, the camping outfits with all the merit badges, everything but the simple fact that it was all over pretty quick and that my son hadn't cried much, which was all I really cared about back then. I actually hadn't been all that keen on circumcision to begin with. It had been Kathy's idea. "He should look like you," she said. "For his sake I hope he doesn't," I joked. "You know what I mean," she said. "This world's confusing enough as it is. And they look like earthworms if you don't. Ew." Then I went online and checked what the anti-circumcision crowd had to say, and it didn't take long to figure out they were nuts. One lady even said, "I only judge the act, not the person," which is bullshit, because an act can't exist without a person doing it, so if you're judging, at some point somebody's got to take the blame. I know you're not supposed to make your mind up based on what kinds of people are on what side, but I just can't get behind abstractions. People who pretend not to be judgmental are the most judgmental people of all—hippies, Christians, teachers—and to be honest, I wasn't all that interested in washing my son's foreskin every single night. Talk about the warrens.

"Okay," I told Kathy, "you win."

"Mark," she said, "this is not a game. No one wins."

I yeah-yeahed her at the time, but now it's starting to sink in. Like I said, I'm slow. I miss things.

Yesterday was Bob's first birthday. We had a few other toddlers over and let them crawl all over the place, which we'd spent the whole morning baby-proofing and making extra clean, meaning photo-shoot clean. Jake and Alex couldn't come, but we understood. Weekends are short enough without all the extra traveling and crying.

Before people showed up, while Kathy and I hid small, sharp, and toxic things, I found the foreskin bottle on the mantel and figured what the hell.

Outside, it was cold and gray. I settled on a spot beneath our rhododendron, its leaves curled up tight from the frost. The ground was so hard I had to stab at it with my trowel, which eventually bent and would've broken off if I had dug any deeper. The foreskin was wrapped in bloody gauze and hard, like an old man's toenail clipping. I put it in the ground and covered it up with dirt. Then I figured I was supposed to say something, but I more or less slept my way through Sunday school and couldn't even remember what came after *Baruch atah Adonai.* Some kind of Jew I am. So I figured I had to come up with a prayer of my own. "Be a good man," I said aloud, looking up at the sky, and right away my voice got small. I tamped down the dirt. "Be a good man," I said again. "Don't be afraid," I said when the dirt was tamped down. And for a change I didn't try to hold it in. I just let the tears fall down my face and into the ground where I'd buried a tiny, dead part of my son. I didn't care who looked. Or how foolish it might've looked if they did: a fat man in wintertime, with his knees in the dirt and a bent trowel in his hand, weeping like a girl. "Don't be afraid," I said once more, for luck, and put the trowel in my back pocket. I wiped my hands on my pants. It was quarter past, and the guests were on their way. I was a mess, but it's not like they'd notice if I took too long to change.

(......)

A TACO JOINT YOU COULD TELL USED TO BE AN IHOP: WARWICK'S Quaker Lane, Rhode Island's longest just-like-anyplace-elseish stretch, is filled with these franchise ghosts. Late in the first semester of freshman year, my roommate—the endlessly midwestern Christian Whitman—and I went out for some all-you-can-eat fajitas at a now-defunct Mexican chain that's since been an Allstate Home & Life, then a Hold Everything, and now a who knows what. About midway through our meal Christian looked up from his skillet and considered for a moment the huaraches and blanket tunics and bullfighting posters adorning the restaurant's stucco walls. "We have a place just like this in ——ville/ton/Falls," he said. "It's called Chi-Chi's." I set down my knife and fork, pushed away my plate, and, into a napkin bearing the newly trademarked Declaration of Salsafication, wept.*

*For the record, there are only three other times in my life when I have felt, in public, so suddenly, acutely, and *inexplicably* sad:

1. Five years old, at a Hafkin reunion at a family restaurant in southern Florida, when, well into in our sixty-seven-minute wait for lunch (Father should've never bought me that stopwatch), Grandpa Ike noted to no one in particular that the restaurant was now in receivership. "Shame they couldn't make a go of it," he said. Beside him, baby Eli ate tartar sauce from its fluted cup with a knife.
2. Seven, at a matinee of *Rear Window* with my aggrievedly unremunerated sister at the local revival house. Well into the film's final reel, a rumpled dad walked in with his soon-to-be-let-down six-year-old son in tow. I asked Libby, "Did they make them pay full price?" And she said she didn't think so, plus, "Wait! So what?" and, "What do you care? Freak . . ."
3. Nine, and trick-or-treating along with Eli and our old man, as Libby—newly ashamed of her Pocahontas (or was it Tiger Lily?) costume—had backed out at the last minute. I was Frankenstein, and Eli was the monster we all call Frankenstein. Suddenly drafted into duty, our old man—nine o'clock drunk at six—had shot up from the den chaise longue, girded his loins with a bedsheet, affixed some Concords to his head with duct tape, and strapped on an apron. "Look," he said through clenched jaw. "Jim Bacchus! Get it?" We didn't, of course, and neither did the car full of sports fans that almost ran us over as we, hand in hand in hand, weaved our way down Angell, but that didn't stop him from shaking his feather-duster thyrsus at them and shouting, "This has happened to every boy! It happened to me when I was your age!" I let go and hung back

at what felt like a plausibly deniable distance, pretending to count my Mounds and Snickers, while Eli gripped our father's fist.* "You're not alone!" my old man shouted into the night.

*He used to pull our hands from our pockets and squeeze. I yanked mine back every time, until one day he stopped reaching for it. But he grasped hard, and at odd angles, and sometimes it hurt.

Kids will become friends or enemies for next to nothing: Oh, I don't know. Legos go a long away. Taste is everything.* Every night after dinner, my old man and I used sit on the couch and pore through visual encyclopedias together. We held the book on both our laps and took turns pointing out our most and least favorite items on each page. Sometimes, when he wasn't too far gone, we'd even get into why.

See again my freshman-year roommate, Christian, a self-described Jeffersonian Democrat. Paired via computer, we got along for as long as we did because we both liked Coke sans ice, LP covers that literalized their titles, and barker-like rock hits that welcomed their listeners ad nauseam. As we unpacked, we all but hugged.

*It was a good run. But midway through spring semester Whitman walked in on me busily copying onto a legal pad subtitles from a frozen frame of the French version of *Three Men and a Baby*. I was working on a paper comparing its cultural assumptions with those of its American remake.* The shaky but unmistakable image upon which I had paused just so happened to be a full-frontal shot of a micturating infant girl. Whitman froze at the door and I in my chair. I fumbled for the remote while he squinted at the screen, then at me, then back at the screen before excusing himself with a quick jut of his jaw and slam of the door. Campus Housing workers arrived the following afternoon to move Whitman's few belongings—he kept what little he owned in a locked steamer trunk—to an undisclosed location at the far end of campus. One of the student workers, whom I recognized from intramural badminton, told me that Whitman had not only been moved to a single free of charge, but he had also asked for and received the perfect 4.0 mythically reserved for a suicide's roommate.

*I know, I know, but it was either this or a paper concerning Emma Bovary's eye colors.

Foster: A backwoods Rhode Island hamlet that singsongishly shares its underperforming school district with neighboring Glocester. Given their propensity to cancel school over what to the rest of the state seems little more than a light dusting, Foster-Glocesterites are considered a bunch of goldbricking candyasses. But I found out the hard way that this microclimatic effect is real when I was forced, in seventh grade, to extend an already overlong sleepover at the Chevaliers'—twins who, by the time we dug out on Monday afternoon, liked me even less than they had on Saturday morning, which wasn't much.*

The sleepover had been their mom's idea. They were new to Fox and needed a little push. From afar, I must have seemed a safe bet. But at some point early Monday morning I clogged their upstairs toilet. (Overnights are hard, especially when any combination of eggs, cured pork, and dairy has been consumed. Weekend breakfast at the Chevaliers'? Something called cheesy hamlettes.) The water cresting, I reached down into the clogged toilet bowl with a Charmin-wrapped fist and retrieved the turds. I then threw them and my rapidly disintegrating t.p. mitt out the second-story crank window and into the gutters of the semi-attached garage, where I figured they likely wouldn't be discovered until late spring, at which point any memory of my gassy little visit would have been suppressed by all parties. Unfortunately, the older of the two stools rattled off the gutter's edge and into the driveway, where it was found later that same day by either Marc or Eric (I never could tell them apart)—as, true to their Canuck roots, the twins proved not only enthusiastic shovelers but capable scatologists.

*Predicting sleepover/*trayf*-related constipation, I packed the jar of pickled beets at which my hosts would turn up their noses. At least there was no point in kicking myself for saying no thanks to their corn.

TV killed what little imagination I might've had . . . : While our parents raised us in what they took to be a TV-less home, every night I spent a good chunk of the early a.m. in the closet under the stairs, watching muted static on a five-inch black-and-white the property's previous owner had left behind. Grandpa Ike, meanwhile, kept color sets in every room but the john, the one place where he insisted on a little peace and quiet. So when spending Saturdays over at our grandparents', no matter what the weather, Eli and I glued ourselves to Channel 56's *Creature Double Feature*, which showcased back-to-back monster movies* and featured, as its theme music, a truncated version of Emerson, Lake & Palmer's "Toccata."

*Which only created yet another rift between Eli and me. Eli loved man-size monsters like Dracula and the Wolf Man, and

I, monster-size monsters like Mothra and Mechagodzilla. This disagreement extended to our playtime, as Eli always wanted to dress up* while I preferred to set up figures here and there and manipulate them like a god.

*I'm not sure he ever outgrew it. In college, as a member of the Society for Creative Anachronism, Eli fought his mock battles clad in the same one-shoulder leopard-skin pelt in which he would also accept his diploma. Coen the Barbarian, he called himself—exiled half brother of Onan and rightful heir to the Throne of Nemesis.

Individual Artist Project Grant Proposal (Dance/Performance) Rhode Island State Council on the Arts

Project Title: *Neoteny* (A Burlesque)

Vivian Goddard

Project Description, 9/11/98

THE RED CURTAIN RISES TO REVEAL A HOT WHITE SPOTLIGHT shining on an otherwise darkened stage. Two figures approach from stages left and right, barely visible—black silhouettes against a black backdrop. They step into the light and meet: boy and girl, naked but for clinging black swimsuits; their lean bodies glazed in droplets of water, their hair slick with it. The spotlight pulls back to reveal the silhouetted smokestacks and mills and water towers behind them. The girl leans forward, weight on her downstage leg, swiveling a bit at the hip. She bats her long, thick lashes at the boy, whose face is now lit by a smaller spot of red-gelled light. The white spot catches a glinting something or other running along the girl's upstage thigh. The boy's jaw is set firm, but his shoulders shake. He reaches for the girl's crotch to grasp this glinting, dangling thing; he snatches it, pulls out a red-tipped tube, and holds it up by its string. The girl gasps, and the lights flood crimson. They freeze. The lights dim, then grow golden, russet tinged with Magic Hour pink. On the sound system, strings swell softly. The girl reaches out and closes her hand over the boy's and opens her mouth to sing: *"I've got the world on a string / I can make the rain go / got that string wrapped round my fin- / -ger."* She opens the boy's fist and takes the tampon. She whips it around and around like a lasso until the short tube telescopes into an arm-length, red-tipped cane. She dances about the boy, twirling it, serenading him. *"What a world, what a life, I'm in lo-o-o-ve!"* The lights cut, and the stage plunges into darkness. The brass blasts loud and plosive. The lights come back up and reveal the girl, now wearing white tails and silk top hat. A bejeweled red satin catsuit clings to the boy's body. The whole stage glows with rich, golden light as the black curtain rises and two curving rows of white marble stairs lower. Two by two, seven-foot anthropomorphic tampons—cotton-covered tubes out of which stick men's legs clad in red fishnet stockings and Lucite stripper heels—stream from a door at the top of the stairs. They form a horseshoe around the boy and girl. The strings swell and the saxophones honk and the trombones blare and the trumpets squeal, squeal, squeal! The horseshoe widens, out rolls a long red carpet, and the boy and girl walk out along it—dressed now in wedding white and black-tie black—white-gloved hand in white-gloved hand. The smokestacks no longer appear in silhouette and now reveal themselves to be, when lit, big-city skyscrapers. They meet at the center of the tampon horseshoe and kiss. Pickle-bucket-size period cups brimming with red corn syrup are lowered from ropes and dumped onto their heads. But the young lovers just kiss on—oblivious, dripping blood, their eyes shut. A four-foot-square card lowers in front of them. Painted on it, a bloody splotch the shape of a valentine heart, and written below in finger-painted streaks:

THE END

(......)

Tampons: According to Eli, the boys in his class didn't know the difference between these and their applicators, calling them both beach whistles. "Why do girls constantly remove them out of doors?" Jake asked.* "That's not how it works, idiot," Alix said. Slepkow wanted to be invisible instead of red. Viv, meanwhile, was long gone. *See?* You could almost hear her say.

> *How this subject even came up is anyone's guess, let alone on the very first day of school. But my brother always did like to wing it. "So," he'd start, ten minutes late and somehow wet, "where were we? Alix?"

The End: Not so fast. But what do I know?*

> *When us Blackall boys* weren't reading or playing by ourselves or, later, watching whatever was on, we passed the time with games of rock-paper-scissors, at least until Eli saw fit to devise a fourth shape—the hole—into which all the other three items fell. You could throw it only once, but that's all it took.

*Look, Libby, how hard I've tried to leave you out of it. I've gone to absurd lengths! You can count on one hand how many times your name's come up. You don't have to believe me. Just trust me, okay? I'm trying my best for a change.

The Quaker Guns

Hank LaChance

My foster kid showed up at the condo carrying a blue gym bag and a grease-stained box with the flaps tucked under.

Phyllis held the door open. "Hank," she said, "this is Carlos."

He was shorter than I pictured. "You're shorter than I pictured," I told him. Couldn't tell how old he was supposed to be. Phyllis had said sixteen, but he could've passed for twelve.

Phyllis is my late wife's sister, and Carlos was her cleaning lady's kid. His mom was out of town because it was going to take at least three months to fix Phyllis's house after some nut had driven into it. With no house to keep all of a sudden, Carlos's mom moved to Jersey, where she had family and there was work. But her kid had won some kind of scholarship at this fancy-pants Quaker school for being sharp and brown, and his mom didn't want to make him start all over again with only a month left till summer. Seeing as how I had room, Phyllis asked me. It was the kind of thing that would have been hard to talk my late wife, Liza, out of saying yes to, so fine, I said. Okay. So Carlos wasn't really a foster. But what else can I call him? I've got to call him something. A guest? The son of my late wife's sister's employee? Some kid? He's his own situation.

"Carlos is from Pawtucket," said Phyllis, looking at him in a way I couldn't imagine he cared for, but he seemed not to notice.

"Central Falls," Carlos said. Kid's glasses made his eyes the size of walnuts.

"Central Falls," Phyllis repeated, like it was the goddamned UN all of a sudden. "He's Colombian," she said, pronouncing all the *o*'s. "American," she added. "Colombian *American.*"

I reached out my hand to shake his, but Carlos held on to his box. I clapped him on the shoulder instead, and he almost lost his footing. Maybe he'd stepped in some of that goose shit on the way from the car. He leaned into the doorjamb and raised the box with his right knee.

"I'm from Central Falls, too," I said. "Not much of a hockey town anymore, huh?"

Phyllis shot me eyes and jowls. Like her sister, Phyllis looked older when she disapproved of something you said. But whose house gets driven into twice, and by the same exact nut, is what I'd like to know.

"I don't like sports," Carlos said to his box.

"Hank, why don't you help Carlos with his things?"

I tried to take the box, but Carlos just tightened his grip. I didn't blame him: kid had his life in there. Bouncing around like that, two hundred miles from his mom and who knows how many from wherever he was really from.

Phyllis had mentioned something about Carlos's "not putting much stock in community," which is how she talks, but that's okay: I could give two for it myself. Liza always wanted a kid. You can say *too little, too late*, all you want, or some good it does now, but when can't you say that? It wasn't my fault the condo hadn't turned out like I planned.

Canada geese. My pond was lousy with them. That ham-and-egger Realtor must've cleared the assholes out of there with his car horn right before he showed it, paid someone to rake up their shit.

And all along I thought the place was cheap on account of the two hundred-year floods they'd had in the five years since they built it, which I never told Liza about. Every five minutes she'd've asked me if I really wanted to sink our retirement into this ticky-tack just on account of some man-made pond I all of a sudden wanted to look at. Old gal was shrewd for a Quaker.

And before you get all worked up about me calling my late wife old gal, you ought to know that Liza used to get a real kick out of it. Phyllis, for one, never got how her sister and I liked to joke. "You can't know what's stuck to the bottom of a couple's pot," Liza told her once. Phyllis made just about the least Quaker face you can imagine, and I imitated it in her blind spot. "Hank doesn't like metaphors," Liza said, winking at me.

Liza died from dehydration, of all goddamned things: we both thought thirst only killed you at sea or in the desert. I have a young, gay, and sportsy niece who carries a squeeze bottle of filtered tap water with her everywhere she goes, and I used to give her a hard time about it, but she hasn't once told-me-so. I also used to work with this chucklehead named Georgie, who called Bigfoot "that guy" and the Loch Ness Monster "that other guy," and who once called into work thirsty. We all gave him hell about it, and I guess I owe him an apology too. But at this point I might as well fly a banner around the state. *LOOK, I'M SORRY. HAPPY NOW?*

While Phyllis poked around, I showed Carlos to the spare room off the kitchen. I had plans to turn it into a workshop, but that could wait till school let out. I was sleeping in the guest room because the master bedroom was filled with boxes of Liza's things and I wasn't ready to get into all that just yet. Liza held on to matchbooks and pamphlets. Restaurant mints. Funeral programs for people she didn't even like. The wood was raw in the spare room, and there was only a little crank window way up high, but it wasn't so bad. I would've loved digs like these at his age.

"You can set this place up however you like," I said.

Carlos ran his fingers along a knotted pine stud, winced, bit out a splinter.

"This cot unfolds," I said, unfolding the cot.

Carlos looked around, peered into the closet. It was too shallow for pants and shirts, but perfect for cans. I think it was supposed to be a pantry. There's no such thing as a spare room these days. It's always a pantry or study or solarium or mudroom. Carlos stood there holding his box until I left him to himself. Fine with me. A man needs his privacy.

Phyllis was in the kitchen smelling milk and asking about coffee, which meant she wanted to talk. I said something quick about Sanka in the cupboard and mugs in the sink, and snuck out back.

As expected, the geese were a stone's throw from the patio, so I grabbed a handful of pebbles out of the planter and chucked it at them. I couldn't see their eyes, but I knew they were staring at me. Two, three times a day, at least, I'd run out there, blasting a boat horn at them and swinging a mop over my head like King Phillip. But they always came back. We kept up this song and dance for months. Now what? I threw the rest of the rocks, but the geese kept on milling and honking and picking nits like they owned the place.

"Scram, shitheads," I said, picking up some mulch and throwing that instead. It didn't go very far, so I really leaned into my next throw and slipped on a green question mark of goose shit slicked with rain. I landed on my ass and felt the landing in my teeth.

The alpha goose lowered his head and started bobbing it. He opened his beak and hissed at me. Then he spread his wings and started to charge. I ran back inside and got the slider closed just in time for him to run into it headfirst. He flapped his wings. I gave him the finger and shut my blinds.

My back killed, but my back, always for shit, had gone out for good when I took a tumble at work, which is how I could afford the condo in the first place. After twenty-five years of running shipping and receiving for Hasbro, I wound up with a pretty good settlement, plus TDI—what we used to call Italian Retirement. I'm French-Canadian, but that doesn't mean I haven't picked up a trick or two about how things work along the way.

But as far as the geese went, I was fresh out of ideas. It had been five long months, and I'd tried nearly everything: road flares, scarecrows, hot pepper, you name it. Only a nut does the same goddamn thing over and over.

Groundskeeping's hands were tied on account of the DEM, and I didn't find out about egg oiling soon enough. (You coat the eggs in oil, and they won't hatch. Then they blame the place and move on. A little Mazola does the trick. But past a couple weeks, there's laws.) Also, Liza made it pretty clear she would never forgive me if I hurt the little s.o.b.'s. "I want no harm to come to those geese," she said in her Quaker Meeting voice, which is a flat, I'm-only-just-saying voice. It didn't help that she was from Connecticut. "These birds are lost, Hank," Liza'd say, all Connecticut Quaker–like, whenever I so much as put my boots on. I tried to tell her they weren't lost, just taking advantage, but Liza wouldn't hear of it. You give someone a part-time job, a kind heart, and a view, and before you know it, they turn into Marlin Perkins. Once, she even swerved off the road to miss hitting a squirrel with no tail. "Come on," I said when we got off the shoulder and going again. "No tail is natural selection." On the way back home she focused on the slow-moving road, eyes peeled for critters.

Liza's doctor was one of these young bucks who don't put much stock in a woman's pain. Her checkups might as well have been drive-throughs. Phyllis thinks we should sue, but I told her we both live decently, so what for? To teach him a lesson, she says. I said there's only one lesson, but it can't be taught and he'll learn it soon enough. We all do. Besides, it's me who should have paid better attention.

Anyway, by the time Carlos showed, I didn't know whether to shit or go blind.

Liza'd been making noises about foster kids for some twenty-odd years before this Carlos thing fell into my lap, ever since the doctor told us my sperm didn't have pointy enough hooks. I had no idea the little fuckers were even supposed to have hooks. Liza wanted to blame it on off-gases, but you can't blame everything on what you do. That's just what work smells like these days. And adoption wasn't in the cards, what with my real kid already out there and me having long since missed my chance to tell Liza about him, so I just told her I didn't believe in it.

By the time we met—Liza and me—my son was, what, eleven and change? And I hadn't seen him in as many years. At that point it didn't even have a thing to do with what kind of kid he was, though if I was being honest, I could guess what kind he'd turn out to be. Things moved real quickly between Liza and me, and before I knew it, we were married, and I couldn't tell her all that stuff without looking like a real asshole. Not telling someone something is the worst kind of lie, because you don't even give them a chance to tell you you're full of shit. That's the problem with meeting someone late in life. You know exactly how lucky you are.

He must be almost thirty by now, my son. Look, it makes me sick to think about, but I mailed checks every other week till he hit eighteen. At this point he wants nothing to do with me, and I don't blame him. Whoever he is, he's his own man.

Last I saw him was at his mother's funeral, when I snuck in the back. I went up to him, after. He looked like a photo of me I had forgotten all about. "Rob?" I said.

He squinted.

"It's me, Hank. LaChance. I'm . . . I'm your—"

"I know who you are. But I don't know you. And you don't know me."

My neck tightened, then my shoulder. "Okay. That's okay. I just, I'm . . . I just wanted to tell you how sorry I am."

"You are."

"About your mother. About . . ." I put out my hand, and he just looked at it, then back at me. I nodded and left.

I guess I can see now that Liza wasn't really settling in all that well. After moving from School Street, we spent the first couple weeks getting the new place squared away. Sure, I saw the geese, but figured they'd be heading north soon enough. Little did I know that migration's a thing of the past, what with weather change and all. Far as they're concerned, the New England suburbs are spring year-round.

I didn't have much of a nest egg—and neither did Liza—and knew this was the last move before my very last one. But not hers. I thought for sure I would go first.

We had to get rid of a lot of stuff to fit everything, but eventually Liza found a spot for her hunt table and the davenport—which is what she called a couch—and her figurines. It was tight in there, but it felt like home. Did to me at least.

But Liza did a hell of a lot more sitting in the new condo. She'd sit in the breakfast nook mostly, and also on the davenport, but never on the patio, which actually looked out onto something, unlike the nook, which looked at a wall decorated with a wreath of dry corn. "What's so interesting about that corn?" I asked her.

"Oh, let me be," she said, and went back to staring.

"I just want to know what you see in it, is all."

"You can't take every last thing apart, Hank. Honestly!"

"Take what apart? I only take apart things I'm trying to fix."

"What is there to fix?"

She had never been what you'd call a big sitter, Liza. She used to stand, mostly—hover. But now, in the condo, it was all she could do to stand in front of the stove long enough to fix a decent meal, let alone make the trip to Almacs for groceries.

I even asked her, once—what the trouble was. I was going through our boxes of books, looking for my encyclopedia, and Liza was sitting in the parlor staring at the wall. We still hadn't decided what to hang there: I was keen on a nineteenth-century nautical map, the kind with beige water, but Liza had wanted this one oil painting her sister had done of a fat, naked gal running through a field of wildflowers. Phyllis painted only fat, naked gals doing different things.

I walked over to the davenport, patted Liza on the knee.

"How you settling in?"

She looked up and closed her eyes at me. Hid her lips to smile. "I'm fine, Hank."

"Hell, I know you're fine, Liza. I asked how you're settling."

She took my hand and pressed it into her knee.

"You want to hang that painting Phyllis did there?" I said.

"Some things can only be missed."

"Now what does that mean," I asked. Metaphors were one thing, riddles something else entirely.

"It's okay," she said. Then she let go of my hand and went back to looking at the blank white wall.

Moving is harder on women, that whole nesting instinct. Everything means something to them. So I went back to searching for my *World Books*. I wanted to study what made these shitbirds tick. Liza gave me some long looks while I opened box after box of things we hadn't dealt with yet. I was real careful—unpacking things into stacks and dividing the stacks into rows—but it got her dander up all the same.

"Now what're you into?" Liza asked once I started rifling through the black and lacy underthings she no longer wore.

"I'm just looking for my *World Books*. Wanna read up on geese."

"And you think you'll find them in my bedclothes?"

"Christ if I know. You pack like a maniac."

"I'm tired, Hank."

"I don't know what you're talking about," I said and meant.

"I can't locate my power," she said.

"Well, you still give me a hard time about how I load the dishwasher," I said, smiling.

"It has nothing to do with you or with that. I don't know where I am," she said, and went to go sit somewhere else for a while. I just thought it was one of her metaphors.

I finally found the "C" volume of my 1959 *World Book*s tucked away in a box full of teeth molds and Xmas cards. The Canada geese entry wasn't much use, apart from the bit about their "agnostic behavior." I was gonna make a joke about it to Liza, but figured she wasn't in the mood, which wasn't like either of us, which was the whole problem. So I kept reading. Back then, the assholes were nearly extinct, if you can even believe it. This was when no one saved any kind of animal from anything, except maybe your dog from a burning barn or a bear trap, and even then only if it would've done the same for you. We used to let civilization take its course.

By the time Carlos got the spare room set up, the goslings had all been born. Now there was even more shit. I could barely step off my patio without skating on a rain-slick tangle of turds. Jesus, you'd think they'd waste away to nothing on account of how much they shat. Apparently those ChemLawn treatments didn't so much as make the lawn taste bitter. They were probably pumping it full of vitamins and Spanish fly and Ex-Lax, for all I knew.

But what drove me even more nuts was that right across the road was a perfectly good corporate park for them to call home. The regional headquarters for Bank of America's pond was five times bigger than ours, easy, and surrounded by a hell of a lot more grass. And you can bet all those secretaries and cubiclers would toss them muffin hunks and sandwich crusts on their coffee breaks. But no matter how many times I chased the flock over there, they found their way back to my pond.

A week into his stay, Carlos started spreading out, not doing his homework in the breakfast nook instead of his pantry. He'd sit there with a couple closed books in front of him and chew on his pen awhile, staring at the air between him and the wall. One time his books were still closed but he was sketching on graph paper, crossing things out, redrawing them with a ruler. "Whatcha working on?" I asked.

"Plans."

"What for?"

"Gutters."

"What do you know about gutters?"

"Phyllis made me clean hers once. Up a ladder."

"Oh yeah?"

"These don't need cleaning. You pull a cord, and they dump out."

"Pretty slick," I said, looking down at the sketch, which was mostly cross-outs but had an exploded view of the release mechanism that almost made sense. There was a C-shaped catch connecting the cord to the gutter, but I couldn't tell how you'd reset it. Wet leaves would probably still stick, also, but between Central Falls and Colombia what'd he know from leaves. "This for school?"

"No, people."

"This place doesn't have gutters. They cut corners."

"I noticed," Carlos said, and went back to his sketch.

The last time I saw Liza conscious, I had just come back from Home Depot. I had a roll of chicken mesh under my arm and found her sitting in the breakfast nook, drinking a cup of Sanka. I knew something was wrong when she didn't offer me any. Normally, she'd have already had the Stella D'oro out of the Brisker and everything. Liza went to take a sip of Sanka, then stopped herself. She put the cup back down on the coaster, centered the coaster on the table, straightened the Plexiglas caddy of Sweet'N Low. She whistled a sigh through her nose.

"What?" I said.

She made a face and shook her head. "The geese, all the trips to the Home Depot." I gave her another look, and Liza lowered her voice. "How is that that you have no job and yet you're still hardly here?"

"Goddammit, Liza. If anything, I'm here too much."

She didn't say anything.

"What do you want me to do? You want me to do what?"

"Hank," she said.

You know actors—I mean the real good movie kind, like that one Jewish fellow, or the one who used to be real quiet but now shouts all the fucking time—how they get when they're trying to look blind or stupid? How they look like they honestly can't see what's in front of them? Well, that's how Liza was looking at me. Like I wasn't even there. Then I noticed that for some goddamned reason she was wearing her India rubber boots and had tucked her pants into them like a quahogger. At the time, though, I was so out of sorts that I didn't even wonder what the hell for.

"What the hell, Liza."

"It hurts." Her face aged.

I didn't know what to do. "I try to be good," I said.

"It's not—"

"I watch my salt and sugar. I count backwards like they told me. I picture the horizon."

"It's not about your heart."

"I try now."

"Hank . . ."

"I'm just saying."

"It's not about you. I look out the window and don't know where I am, and now you with those fucking Canadian geese—"

"Canada geese," I said, because I couldn't help it.

Liza steepled her fingers, then pushed her forehead into the steeple, breaking it apart.

My chest knotted. Liza was the only person I trusted who barely swore. I sat down in the breakfast nook, opposite my wife. The cushion sighed beneath me. Liza stood up. She took her cup to the sink and ran it under cold water. We both agreed hot was for real germs. It didn't matter that I was worried more about bills than about ozone or wetlands or whatever—in the end we just liked that in the end we had the same solutions.

"Yeah," I said, still expecting her to tell me how I could help.

Liza opened the kitchen door to the garage, and I caught a quick whiff of oil and naphthalene. Doesn't take long for even a new garage to smell like an old one, I thought. "Don't you think that smells like a real garage?" I asked.

She tossed the empty Sanka can into the recycling bin and shut the door. Then she sat down in the nook and looked up at me with wet red eyes.

"Shit, Liza."

"I really hurt," she said, then doubled over, clutching her belly.

By the time I got Liza to the accident room, she was unconscious. The doctor asked me if she ever drank water.

"Sanka," I said. "Metamucil?"

He frowned a doctor frown and told me she was completely dried up and might need a colon operation. She did. Then she blew up twice her size from staph, went into a coma, and it was all downhill from there.

At some point it occurred to me that Carlos was watching too much TV, even if it was mostly educational. Didn't he have homework? At a school like that? But what did I know from education. So I figured what the hell, and gathered up a stack of procedurals that I had liked and carried them with me into the parlor, where I found Carlos watching something about the Incans or the Mayans. I put the stack down on the coffee table and said, "Here you go, kid. Thrillers."

He leaned to the left to watch his program.

"I like the scenes where the buck gets stopped," I told him, stepping to one side.

He just looked at me.

"Look," I said. "I folded down the corner for each page where the guy takes matters into his own hands for a change."

"That's not how things change."

So I said, "That's why you start another right after."

"But that's the whole problem," he said. "The next one picks up where the last one started, not ended."

So I go, "You could say that about anything, you know."

"In real life, it takes more than one guy," he said, and went back to his program.

"I just try and think of it as one long book I'm never gonna finish," I said, leaving my stack and the room.

Carlos hadn't been around for more than a month before Phyllis called to tell me he might not pass junior year.

"Why the hell not?" I said.

"He's been skipping gym. He and some other boys like to nap in the cloakroom."

"They'd hold him back for sports? Sports!" I could feel my blood. I pictured someplace else. Someplace wide open and far away.

"It's a policy. They said they'd let him make it up if he apologizes."

"There you go."

"He won't apologize."

"That beats everything."

"His adviser says he just shrugs."

"Well, maybe he'd like it better in Newark. Maybe he'd like to go back to Central Falls instead of napping in the goddamned cloakroom."

"This won't help."

"Not sure I care."

"Hank."

"I'll talk to him."

"Please."

"Why'd they call you?"

"I called them."

"What the hell for?"

"Because."

"Because what?"

"I know you."

"What's that?"

"Do you and Carlos talk?"

"Of course we talk!"

"I know you, and knowing you, you don't ever ask him anything."

"I tell him plenty."

"How about how was your week? You don't ask that, I bet."

"Where do you even come from with this crap? Kid needs a place all of a sudden and I took him in."

"You sure didn't ask Liza—"

"Phyllis."

"Look, Hank—"

"You don't start a sentence with *look* when you talk to me. Where do you get the brass to tell me look!"

"Carlos—"

"I'm gonna call that school. I'm gonna straighten things out."

"My sister—"

"Okay," I said, and hung up. I sat back in the nook and looked up at the ceiling fan, noticed some cracks in the tiles at its base. There was a little too much play at low speeds. Maybe I could adjust the motor some.

Carlos was in the parlor, drinking a chocolate soda and watching a program on beavers.

"So what's all this about cutting gym?" I asked.

Carlos shrugged.

"Look, kid, I'm not angry with you. I just want to help grease the skids a little."

"Gym is stupid. They make us climb a rope."

"Gym class is for assholes. But sometimes you gotta think about the big picture."

On TV, a beaver swatted mud with its tail.

"Don't you want to graduate next year?"

Carlos shrugged, his walnuts still fixed on beavers. His goddamn glasses looked like Pacer windshields. No wonder he couldn't climb things.

"Look, I know life dealt you a shit hand, but if you just play your cards, you have a lot of options."

"I want to go to RPI," Carlos said.

I hadn't the slightest idea what he was talking about, but it was the first remotely positive thing to come out his mouth, so I figured I'd humor him. "There you go."

Carlos took a sip of soda.

"Look, is there something else you could do instead of gym—you know, like game clock or something? Equipment manager?"

Carlos nodded. "Fencing."

"Christ, kid, you gotta wear that beekeeper outfit, and isn't it all in French?"

Carlos shrugged.

"Okay, okay. Fencing it is. So all you gotta do is go and apologize to someone and you're all set: no rope, no staying back."

"I'm not going to apologize."

"Why the hell not?"

"I'm not sorry. Gym is stupid."

"Look, you don't have to be sorry, you just gotta apologize."

"I don't apologize when I'm not sorry."

"All right, have it your way. See how much fun junior year is the second time around. The Bill of Rights only gets worse."

"I'll fence, but I'm not going to apologize to anyone about anything."

"It's no big deal. People say they're sorry all the goddamned time. You think they mean it? You say sorry at the market, for christsakes. You say sorry at McDonald's. That's just life."

"Where I come from, you don't say I'm sorry."

"Look, kid, when you talk like that, my mind goes blank."

"Talk like what?"

"When you talk about a place or the people who live in it, instead of about yourself."

"Gotcha."

"Now what is that supposed to mean?"

"That I got it." Carlos took another drink of soda and went back to his nature program. Turned up the volume good and loud with the remote. At this point, those goddamn beavers were making an ungodly mess of what had once been, in all likelihood, a perfectly good creek—drowning saplings, turning land to swamp. I thought about the geese and Liza's ashes, and my shoulder tightened. Took a deep breath, counted backward from six, and let Carlos alone with his show. So what if they held the little prick back, I thought, I'd be shipping his ass to Newark soon enough anyhow. Hell, I'd even send him back to Benefit Street to breathe dust and eat food with nothing in it and go to meetings all weekend long. I had enough to worry about between Liza being gone and these goddamn geese without foster-kid nonsense keeping me up at night. Way things were going, I'd wind up in the accident room for sure. It'd only been two years since I took my last heart attack and still had the sugar and was hardly in the clear.

"Look, I know how it is. How your old man split."

"No. He's dead."

"Oh. Liza would've known that," I said.

"Look," he said, "you don't know me, and I don't like you, so let's just give each other some space."

"I!" I didn't know what to say. "You don't know me, either," I said.

"Sure I do."

"What makes you so sure."

"Because that's all white guys do is talk about who they are and how everybody else should feel."

"I don't tell you anything!"

"Don't have to."

"Well, maybe there's more."

He shrugged. "White is an absence."

"Well, I got a niece who says all us French-Canucks are all part Indian, if you go back far enough. She read it in a book."

He looked at me long enough for me to notice he wasn't blinking.

"It's true!"

"It's also stupid."

I had something else to say, but I forgot it as soon as I opened my mouth, which felt dry all of a sudden. But instead of getting a drink, I walked around the living room twice, then sat down and watched the program with him, which was no longer about beavers, but about aqueducts and how to make them now the way they used to. It was pretty interesting, actually. But Carlos was sitting where I used to sit, and I had a hard time focusing. I could feel my heart everywhere but in my heart.

That night I didn't sleep all that well. I used to think the dead needed an address, and that's why I hadn't cast Liza's ashes like she wanted and instead kept them in a sextant box on the mantel, but now I wasn't sure that I had done the right thing. But I couldn't do it—sprinkle her here and there, like fertilizer. "Like wedding rice," she'd said.

I pictured the wind carrying away scoops meant for the spot where Roger Williams first landed or the Great Swamp or wherever. "Why are we even talking about this!" I said. "You're gonna put *me* in the ground. This'll be your sister's problem. Or else your goddamn nephew's, if he's not too busy."

"Oh, Hank. You'll know what to do."

"I'm going first!"

In addition to not getting buried, Liza also didn't have a funeral. Instead she had a memorial at the Quaker Meeting House. Phyllis set it all up. It was run like one of their meetings, where everybody gets a chance to talk. Some people take too long. Some say dumb things, or things that only sound good and in the end mean way less than the dumb things. But that's just how it works.

I didn't get up to speak, because I didn't have anything to say—not to these people, most of whom I didn't know from Adam. Phyllis also had a hard time saying her piece, or her peace, or whichever. I mean, physically. She couldn't find her voice. She got out her own name—which is just how they do things, I gather—and the part about being Liza's sister, but that was it. Nothing else came out. We all waited. Phyllis was sitting next to me. I looked up at her and put my hand on her back—without any strength; I wasn't holding her up or anything—and waited along with everybody else. It felt funny, my hand on her back, and even funnier when it slipped to her hip, then quickly back to her back, and I'm not sure it helped any, but I had to do something. "Sorry," she mouthed, and sat down so fast that my hand got stuck there, between her back and the pew. She gave me a flat, trembly smile, and I gave her one back. I let my hand go numb behind her, and we just sat and listened to everybody talk about my wife.

At some grayish point before dawn I got out of bed and drank my coffee on the patio in a snow hat and parka. At the pond's rim, the geese were still asleep, their necks tucked into their round gray bodies. They looked like rocks smoothed by years and years of falling water. I watched them stir awake, their black necks rising. At some point I heard Carlos microwave bacon in the kitchen and then leave to go catch his bus. How many servings of pork should a kid his age eat a week? Six? Seven? Did it matter where his ancestors were from?

Once the geese were up and doing their thing, I went back into the house, put on my tie and sweater-vest, and drove down to that Quaker school to try and square things away for Carlos. Probably should've given the kid a lift, but I didn't want to be a goddamned chauffeur.

I'd read enough books to know that you got to start at the top, so I'd made an appointment with the headmaster, who wore a suit and tie but told me to call him Ned. His office smelled like Christmas cookies and shaving cream, and he called me Henry, but I didn't correct him. What the hell is it with Quakers and first names? I told Ned that Carlos was real keen on fencing all of a sudden and wanted to graduate on time. He said something about citizenship, and apologies being an integral part of their school culture. I told him *sorry* wasn't a word in this kid's vocabulary and tried to make a point about how he grew up, but it was no use. Truth be told, I didn't know enough about Central Falls these days or Colombia at any point, let alone Carlos, to make that particular point. So Ned told me that if Carlos didn't apologize to the athletic director, he would have to make up his credits over summer break, and even then he might not graduate on time and could possibly lose his scholarship. I had originally thought the kid was being a pain in the ass about all this, but I was starting to come around to his way of thinking.

"Well, it would seem we're at an impasse," Ned said.

"What the hell is it with you fucking Quakers anyway? For a bunch of people who won't fight wars and send kids home early on Wednesday and sit around having meetings all weekend long, you're stubborn as hell."

"Henry, I would appreciate it if you lowered your voice and checked your language. This is not a loading dock, and I'm not a Quaker."

"And that's another goddamned thing. You think that just because you use someone's first name, you're being democratic. Well I got news for you, *Ned*, democracy is something you earn." And I walked out of his office. Looked like Carlos was gonna have to spend next year taking boiler room Civics in some Central Falls shithole. I never was much of a diplomat.

I broke the news to Carlos over a supper of hot dogs and sauerkraut—the only meal I could really manage, apart from Cup-a-Soups. "Well, looks like you're gonna need to take gym over the summer. I talked to that Dubberford character, but got nowhere. Might as well've tried reasoning with a box of threepenny nails."

Carlos shrugged. "I don't like him either."

"I can see where you're coming from. He's a real ham-and-egger."

Carlos nodded and took a big bite of hot dog. We sat there for a while, eating and not talking. Carlos chewed with his mouth open but was decent company just the same. I topped off his coffee without him even asking, like they do at the restaurants I like, and then did the same for myself. I had the fan on low to clear out some of the smoke—burned the dogs a little—and the ceiling made a gritty noise as the blades turned slow and wobbly. I got up and walked over to the icebox and pulled out a couple 'Gansetts and cracked them open for Carlos and me. "A man can't have too many beverages," I said, and went on to alternate cold, foamy pulls of beer with sips of hot black coffee. Carlos did the same. What the hell, I thought, it's not like I fixed the kid a highball. "What the hell," I said after a while. Carlos nodded, and his glasses slipped down his nose. Turned out he had normal-size eyes under there.

Later that evening I was sitting on the patio eating mixed nuts and looking at sliding-door night glare when Carlos came up behind me. "What is it?" I said to his reflection.

"I've got an idea, about the geese."

"Yeah?" I turned around.

"I saw a show, and it gave me an idea."

My heart pinched. The valve, I think. I took a deep breath.

"Let's hear it," I said, and he handed me this sketch, which I've kept.

We waited until Sunday to try it out. The inside of his box smelled like onions and something else. Eraser crumbs. I had covered up the SlepCo logo with electrical tape. "They can't read," Carlos said. "You don't know that," I said. "These shitheads are going to bury us all." I crouched and stuck my left arm—sheathed in what had once been the right leg of Liza's best black nylons—through a hole cut in the top of the box. The paint that Carlos smeared at the stocking's ankle felt damp and sticky against my wrist, but we both felt the white dewlap really sold it. I used my right arm to steady myself because my knees have been bone on bone since Nixon went to China. (Hockey takes its toll.) At first I could just make out patches of light and dark through the slit Carlos had cut for me, but my eyes soon adjusted. Carlos snuck in behind me, sliding his arms out the armholes he had made in the sides of the box and into the gray satin nightgown wings he had stapled there. He gave the wings a quick flap, and the box rose around us.

"Knock it off, willya, kid?" I whispered through clenched teeth, clamping down on the snow goose call we bought at Wal-Mart. They don't make Canada goose calls, but a honk's a honk in my book.

Carlos's Junior Engineers belt buckle dug into my tailbone as we walked toward the pond, and I could feel his breath on the back of my neck. Smelled like sleep and breakfast. We weren't twelve paces from the patio, and I'd already broken a sweat. Carlos kept catching the heels of my shoes, stepping them flat and almost off.

"Give me some room," I said.

Carlos pulled away a hair and flapped those satin wings some more. Damp, cool air rose into the box, and I tried not to lose my footing in the slick muck of the sloping pond bank. This goddamn getup better work, I thought.

The geese massed in a tear shape along the pond. The ladies encircled the goslings and the bulls encircled the ladies. The goslings were the color of dead dandelions and cheeped as we approached. The bulls looked up at us, this crouching, four-legged Frankenstein goose with silvery wings, and backed away with confused little honks.

"Stop here, Carlos." I stuck my free hand into what probably wasn't mud. Then I swooped my black-stockinged arm swiftly down and slowly up again. Slapped that hand bill open and shut and open and shut again and blew hard into my goose call. There was a still moment. They stared at us. One of the bigger bulls took a few steps toward me and started to open his wings and straighten his neck, so I lashed out my arm like a snake and Carlos flapped the wings stiffly. The lead bull scooted back to the circle's edge. They were still and quiet again.

"Okay, show 'em the other pond," Carlos whispered over my shoulder. Then he gave the satiny wings a slow and no doubt dramatic flapping. The oily cardboard walls expanded and contracted around us while he flapped. I straightened up and blew into the call—a long, determined honk. The geese moved slowly back toward the pond, never taking their eyes off us. I craned my goose-neck arm to the left, toward the road and away from my property. They followed my hand with their beady little eyes. I jerked my arm repeatedly in this direction, watching them snap their necks in sympathy. "Now!" Carlos said. He flapped the wings, and we both turned away from the pond and carefully climbed its bank toward the road. Behind us I could hear wings flapping and the mucky sucking of webbed footsteps and eventually throaty clucks and honks. They were following us up the hill and across the road to Bank of America. Behind me, Carlos laughed somewhere deep in his belly. I clenched my teeth down onto the lip of that snow goose call. Carlos flapped those great gray satin wings again, and the box lifted, and cool air rushed up my back, sore and slicked with sweat, chilling me. The wind picked up, and Carlos held on to the box, pulled it down. I could hear the geese falling in behind us. My heart turned inside out, changed shape. I could feel it all slipping away, the world turning white as ash. I stumbled. The edges of what was in front of me vanished. Carlos leaned in. "You see?" Carlos said, stopping and turning us around. "Look!"

I shook the color back into my head. The geese lowered their necks against the wind and waited. We turned the box back toward Bank of America's pond, dimpling silver in the wind. The geese huddled, waiting. I blew the call again. Their honks and clucks turned to murmurs, then silence. An empty semi shuddered down the road. Then a honking K-car, piled to the roof with newspapers. The wind shifted, and the geese tucked goslings, still yellow in spots, into their wings. They held their ground. They settled in.

(......)

. . . *SOME NUT HAD DRIVEN INTO IT*: UPON IMPACT, THE ROCKS Phyllis had sunk into the sidewalk to protect her house, the next time, bent into a ramp, sending Eli's Volare through her parlor ceiling and into the master bath. "Don't tell my mother," Eli said after EMTs extracted him from the wreck. "She's Jewish." He died seconds later.

. . . *where Roger Williams first landed*: Many assume that the roughly Moshassuck River–bordering Roger Williams National Memorial marks the spot where my father's ninth great-grandfather "What cheered" Providence into being.* But Williams actually landed at Slate Rock on the Seekonk River. Of course the rock in question was, way back in 1877, mistakenly dynamited by city workers excavating the area for artifacts of historical interest.

> *It couldn't have helped that, in the 1970s, the walls and booths of the McDonald's nearest to the Moshassuck depicted Roger Williams and his indigenous hosts in various states of discovery, cooperation, and thanksgiving.* This same

establishment would later become infamous for selling illicit drugs over its counter—Mob pot mostly, but also stepped-on coke. The code phrase was "Remember when Grimace used to be a bad guy *x* years ago?" To which the cashier would respond by slipping into your bag an eight ball of whatever break you felt you deserved that day—indicated by *x*—and ringing you up for anywhere between six and three dozen imaginary Big Macs and any number of apple pies. When the cops busted them in the mid-'80s, their franchise was promptly revoked. The building sat empty for mere weeks—an empty McDonald's is still a McDonald's—before being demolished and replaced by Brown's Copy Center, which was itself replaced by its Job Lab some twenty years later.

*The last time I can remember Eli, our sister, and me all sitting alone together for any length of time was at a booth in this very McDonald's. We were then seven, thirteen, and eleven years old. Our folks were somewhere—Cuddyhunk? Dead already? Had we not been told yet?—so our neighbors Dot and Tod Mortenson had dropped us off on their way to the movies. We ate, looked at the murals, talked about what College Hill must've looked like back in those days, and before long got around to whatever became of the Narragansetts. Libby said we killed them all, and I said, "Nuh-uh, one came to school and told us stories." And she said, "That wasn't a real Indian." So I said, "Was too. He had a pipe and a drum and pants made out of animals he respected." And she said, "Adults pretend to be all kinds of things they're not," and looked away, which was my cue to knock it off unless I wanted a temple flick or baby hair pull, which I didn't. We ate in silence for a while until Eli knocked over the orange soda that only Libby knew to be uncarbonated.

I used too many napkins to sop it up and also spilled some salt. Libby told me I wasn't helping and got back in line to refill Eli's drink. I continued making a slurry of whole milk and tallow-fried fries inside my mouth—too young at this point to identify, let alone mind, the havoc lactose wreaked on my guts—and watched Libby stand there, blowing straight blond hair from her face and shifting her weight from one tanned, Tretorned foot to the other. Libby always did know when she was being looked at, and she knew how to make something as simple as waiting for something look like an ordeal. Then Eli said, "Sometimes I just want to kill myself."

I stopped chewing.

"Sometimes I just feel like I don't want to be where I am."

I swallowed, and it hurt going down. Eli's breath smelled upset even from across the booth, and so did mine, probably, but you can't smell your own. And for the first time that I could remember, I wanted to touch my brother, to just put my hand on his head and brush his short blond hair against the growth because it might feel nice for both of us, so I reached for him. But bent like that, at the waist—already bigger then than it should have been—my throat tightened and turned inside out, and I vomited across the table—fries and milk that still tasted like fries and milk but also bile. Eli exploded into tears, and I said, "I'm sorry, I'm sorry, I'm sorry," over and over again until Libby came stomping back and by the fat of my arm dragged me out front, where I sat while, inside, she did her best to calm Eli down. I sat stock-still until an old guy in a white T-shirt burst through the door, kicked two pigeons into flight, and threw his coffee at the sun. It hung in the sky for what felt like forever.

"I'm sorry," I said to him, and he said, "You're just like everyone else," and I nodded. He ran after a city bus, and I hoped he'd catch it even though it felt as if the part of me that hoped for things had just left my body to chase that rattling bus along with him, like a helpful, hopeful, misunderstood ghost. From somewhere far off came the sound of Styrofoam and coffee exploding against windshield glass, the squeal of tires and brakes, and swerving, honking, and curse words, and then nothing but the louder-than-you-ever-realize drone of a hot, mad city, but also the sounds I couldn't hear and wanted to: Eli crying and Libby hushing and shushing him and telling him everything was going to be all right. And through it all, there I sat, all alone on a brick-faced wall, not moving an inch, but saying sorry to and for everyone as though they could hear me and as though any of it would help. When I was done, I kept still and waited for Dot and Tod, and the inevitable series of irritated honks.*

*What did they go see, the Mortensons? *The Conversation*? No, that would have been at the Showcase, not the Columbus. *F Is for Fake*? Not a broad enough release. *Lancelot du Lac*? Same problem. *Murder on the Orient Express*? Another mall picture. *The Parallax View*? *Young Frankenstein*? Mall, also. What? *The Phantom of Liberty*? *A Woman Under the Influence*? No, and no. Even if the Mortensons were still alive, they likely wouldn't remember. Yet another thing that shouldn't bother me.*

But it's something I could know for sure. What I don't know feels like an absorbed twin. I have dense bones and can write different things with both hands at the same time. Now if I could just figure out the exact date.

All through school they told us that good students use what they know to figure out what they don't, but I'm beginning to wonder if they didn't have it exactly backwards.

*My first night out of prison, I took my father's metal detector over to India Point Park, at the mouth of the Seekonk, hoping to find some old coins or rings or who knows what. Maybe even the flight hat and plugged-up starter pistol Eli buried there when he was six. I rarely visited India Point during park hours, and I figured that by detecting at night, I could avoid the sneering looks of trike-stroller joggers, dog parents, undergrads on dates on swings. Or those of people who thought they knew all about me. People forget that above all else, a voyeur prizes his own anonymity—something in short supply in a town like Providence, where everyone knows everyone else's shit. Even people you've never met think they know you. But bums were fine.

After about an hour of metal detection, I'd found only a couple nickels, a key to nothing, effectively, and a rebus cap from a beer quart that I still keep in my back pocket—it bites me in the ass from time to time—and of which I still can't make heads or tails:

I was about to call it a night when two strangers approached from the left. From where I stood, in the dark—the moon was a toenail clipping and there was my myopia—I couldn't see their faces. But whoever they were, they were themselves, which was all that really mattered, and I couldn't and can't and shouldn't make up anything about them. One stranger wore a black knit hat despite the Indian-summery murk, and the other had hair matted into a hat no one in his right mind would put on his head. They smelled like wine and fire. I swept my detector coil back and forth across the turf in little Turkish moons, trying not to look like I was ignoring them, which I wasn't. Eye contact is hard for me.

"Fuck is that?" asked the actually hatless one.

I swept my crescents, telling myself they were only talking to each other.

"You—what the fuck *is* that!"

"It's a metal detector," I said to the ground. "I'm detecting metal."

"Man," Hatless said, leaning in and poking me in the chest with a finger as hard as rebar. His breath was bitter. "What the fuck is your problem?"

"Shut the fuck up," said Watchcap, slugging his friend in the arm, like a friend, but also for real. "It's his hobby."

Then they both just stood there for a while and watched me not find lost things. We likely all knew I wouldn't. But that didn't mean I couldn't try.*

Acknowledgments

You can't spend fifteen years writing a book and not have more people to thank than space and propriety allow for. But I'm way past looking cool, and there's no guy with a hook, so . . .

Thank you to my two best teachers, always swapping roles of devil and angel on my shoulder: Michelle Latiolais, whose brilliant crits—typed in Courier and signed in Palmer—and opinions on everything from narrative economy (overprized) to unreliable narrators (who's reliable, again?) and even anchovies (don't tell your guests) would show up in a scan of my brain; and Geoffrey Wolff, who taught me everything I know about on-the-page haberdashery and bullshit detection, and who, with his characteristic good humor and filthy sense of it, helped me to weather the respective highs and lows of the 2004 postseason and presidential election.

Thanks, also, to Brad Watson, who showed me how to stick up for what matters; Maile Meloy, who taught me how to let go of what doesn't; and Amity Gaige, who pointed out that the writer I was failing to be back then not only already existed, but had died.

Thank you to all my readers at UC-Irvine: Aaron Miller, Marisa Matarazzo, Mona Ausubel, Michael Andreasen, Zach Braun, Peter Jacoby, Liz Chandler, Michelle Chihara, Kevin Lee, Izzy Prcic, Erin Almond, David Morris, Lauren Coleman, and Christina Byrne; and elsewhere: Matthew Derby, Mira Jacob, Will Allison, Zach Green, and Laura Healy.

An above-and-beyond and how-could-I-possibly-thank-you thank you to my best buddy and writing husband, Matt Sumell.

Thank you to my smart and stalwart agent, Shaun Dolan, who saw what I had here before it was even there, and who literally encourages me, and even buys me lunch.

Thank you to my intuitive, electric, and damn-near omniscient editor, Julie Buntin, without whose help I likely wouldn't be thanking anyone right now. Thanks also to Andy Hunter, Pat Strachan, Jennifer Abel Kovitz, John McGhee, Charlotte Strick, Claire Williams, Zohar Lazar, Natalie Degraffenried, and everyone at Catapult for giving my book a home.

Thanks to everyone who has put me up or hooked me up with a place to write: Jane and Art Salzfass, Travis Alber, Sam Leader, and Stephen Barber. Thank you to UC-Irvine's School of Humanities and the International Center for Writing and Translation for the grant; to the Rhode Island State Council on the Arts for the fellowships. Thanks also to Cristina DiChiera and Mary-Kim Arnold. And to Roberta Rose, Dr. Eric Goldlust, and the entire staff of the Miriam Hospital Urgent Care Center. ("You're working on a book?")

Thanks to my former students and current friends, who have long since closed the maybe-never-existent gap between what I taught them and what they teach me. And also to all the real-life fountain-drinkers, ham-and-eggers, mess-makers, and exes of the actual Providence, Rhode Island. You know who you are, and no, that isn't you, or her, or him, or me, but if you squint maybe you can see our old house from here.

But most of all, thank you to my real family for being unlike my made-up families: my parents, Margery and Milo; mes beaux parents, Leigh et Laurent, et mon beau frère, David; and my wife, Olivia, and my son, Noah, whose love and laughter and wisdom sustain and inspire me.

About the Author

Max Winter is a graduate of UC Irvine's MFA program, and a recipient of two Rhode Island State Council on the Arts Fellowships in Fiction. He has been published in *Day One* and *Diner Journal*. He lives in Providence, Rhode Island, with his wife and son.

MOON HANDBOOKS®

CABO

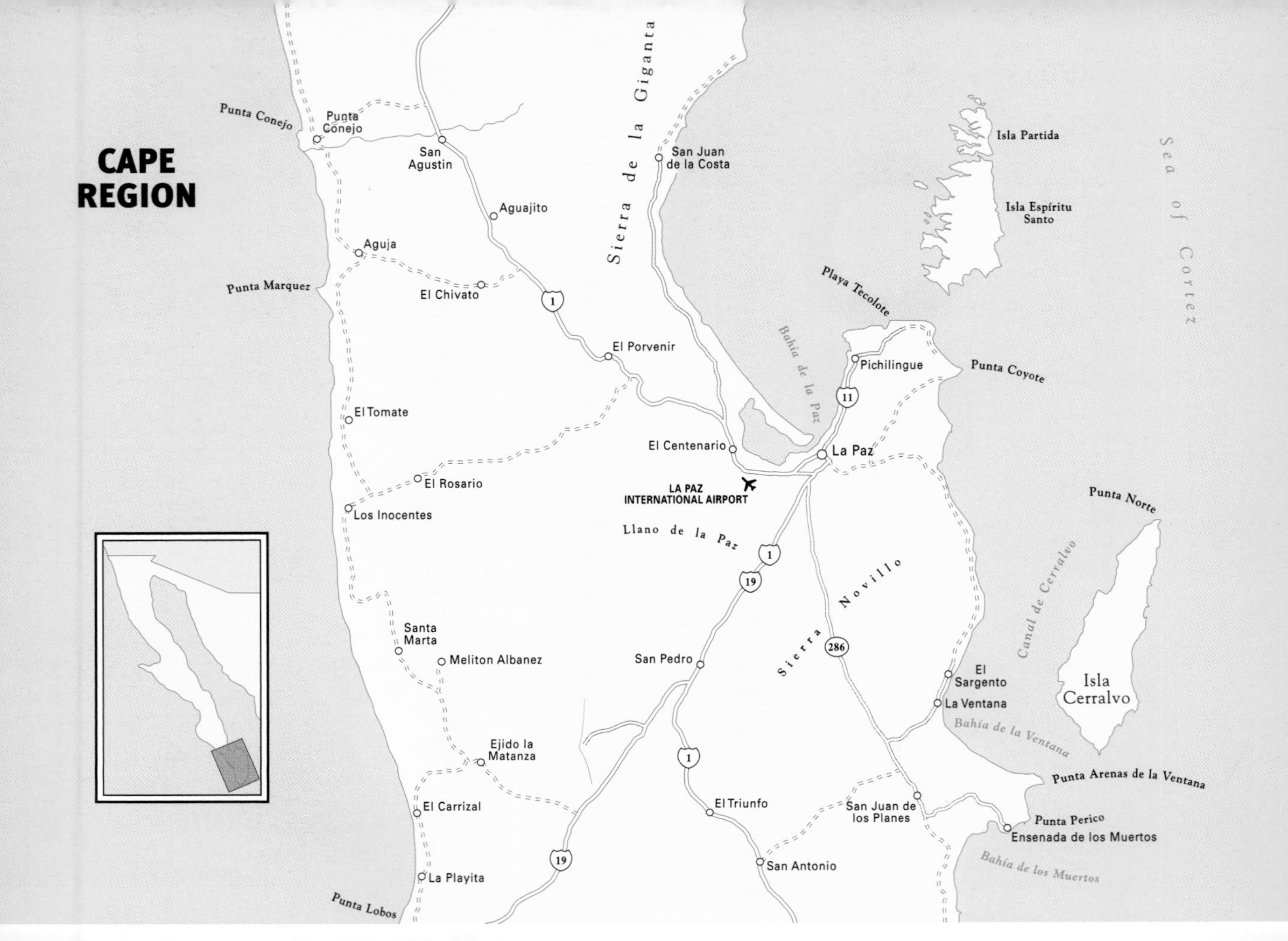

CAPE REGION
Sea of Cortez
Isla Partida
Isla Espíritu Santo
Playa Tecolote
Punta Coyote
Pichilingue
Bahía de la Paz
La Paz
Punta Norte
Canal de Cerralvo
Isla Cerralvo
El Sargento
La Ventana
Bahía de la Ventana
Punta Arenas de la Ventana
Punta Perico
Ensenada de los Muertos
Bahía de los Muertos
Sierra Novillo
San Juan de los Planes
San Antonio
El Triunfo
San Pedro
LA PAZ INTERNATIONAL AIRPORT
Llano de la Paz
El Centenario
San Juan de la Costa
Sierra de la Giganta
El Porvenir
Aguajito
San Agustin
Punta Conejo
Aguja
El Chivato
Punta Marquez
El Tomate
El Rosario
Los Inocentes
Santa Marta
Meliton Albanez
Ejido la Matanza
El Carrizal
La Playita
Punta Lobos
1
11
19
286

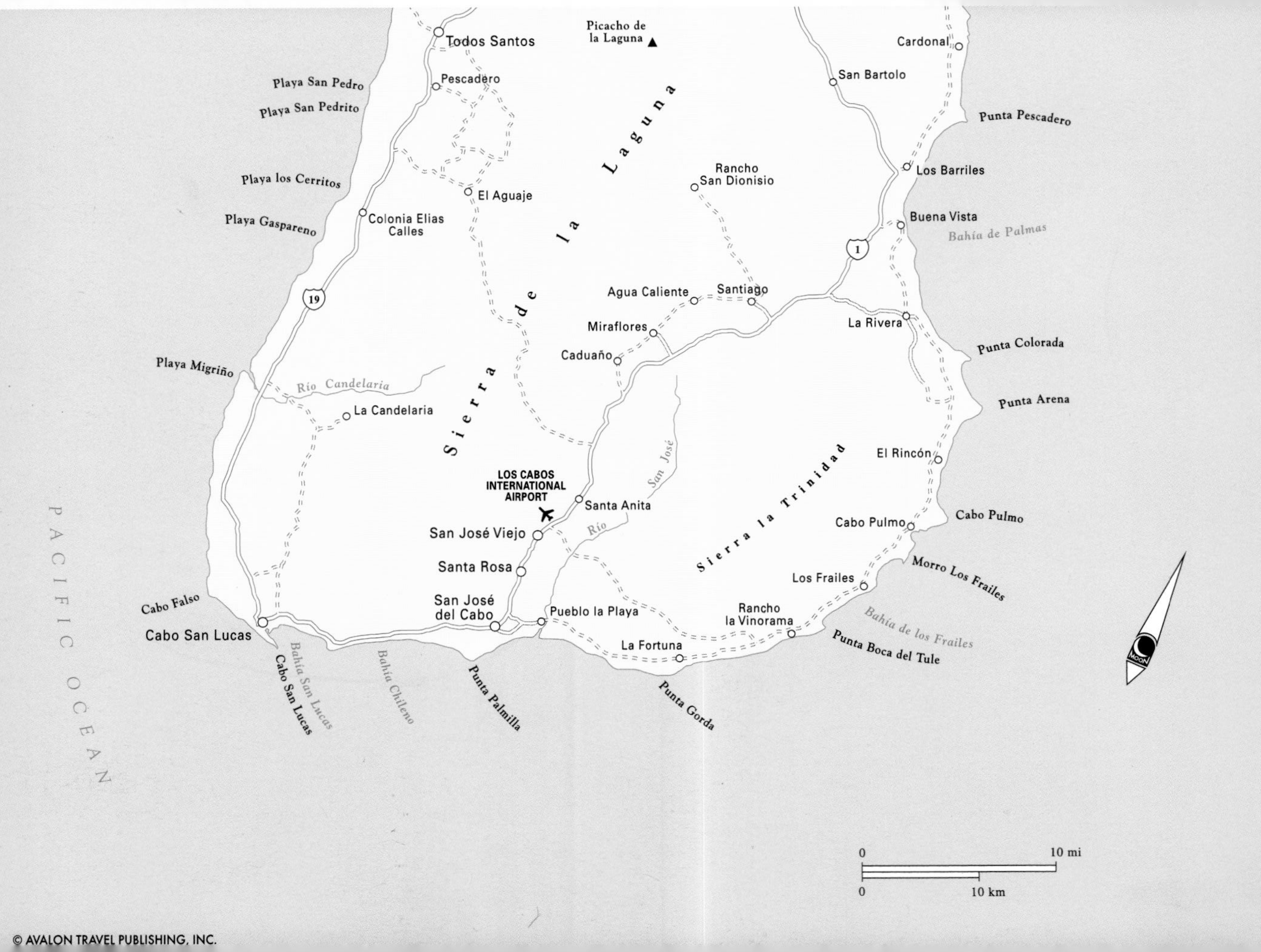
Todos Santos
Picacho de la Laguna
Cardonal
San Bartolo
Playa San Pedro
Pescadero
Playa San Pedrito
Punta Pescadero
Sierra de la Laguna
Rancho San Dionisio
Los Barriles
Playa los Cerritos
El Aguaje
Colonia Elias Calles
Buena Vista
Playa Gaspareno
Bahía de Palmas
1
19
Agua Caliente
Santiago
Miraflores
La Rivera
Caduaño
Punta Colorada
Playa Migriño
Río Candelaria
La Candelaria
Punta Arena
El Rincón
LOS CABOS INTERNATIONAL AIRPORT
San José
Santa Anita
Sierra la Trinidad
Cabo Pulmo
Cabo Pulmo
Río
San José Viejo
Santa Rosa
Morro Los Frailes
Los Frailes
Cabo Falso
San José del Cabo
Pueblo la Playa
Rancho la Vinorama
Bahía de los Frailes
Cabo San Lucas
La Fortuna
Punta Boca del Tule
Bahía San Lucas
Cabo San Lucas
Bahía Chileno
Punta Palmilla
Punta Gorda
PACIFIC OCEAN
0
10 mi
0
10 km

BOUTIQUE
TO CALL